DIRECTED BY KASPAR SNIT

Cary Fagan

Tundra Books

Published in Canada by Tundra Books,
75 Sherbourne Street, Toronto, Ontario M5A 2P9

Published in the United States by Tundra Books of Northern New York,
P.O. Box 1030, Plattsburgh, New York 12901

Library of Congress Control Number: 2006925482

Library and Archives Canada Cataloguing in Publication

Fagan, Cary
Directed by Kaspar Snit / Cary Fagan.

Sequel to: The fortress of Kaspar Snit.
ISBN 978-0-88776-753-1

I. Title.

PS8561.A375D57 2007 JC813'.54 C2006-902092-2

We acknowledge the financial support of the Government of Canada through the Book Publishing Industry Development Program (BPIDP) and that of the Government of Ontario through the Ontario Media Development Corporation's Ontario Book Initiative. We further acknowledge the support of the Canada Council for the Arts and the Ontario Arts Council for our publishing program.

Design: Sean Tai
Typeset in Plantin

Printed and bound in Canada

This book is printed on acid-free paper that is 100% recycled, ancient-forest friendly (40% post-consumer recycled).

2 3 4 5 6 12 11 10 09 08 07

For Sophie,
who waited patiently

And for Emilio and Yoyo,
in friendship

1

THE DINOSAUR WORE GREEN PAJAMAS

I was in the kitchen trying to sneak a cookie when somebody knocked frantically on the door. I opened it and saw Mr. Worthington standing on our step. He looked as if he'd been in a windstorm, or fallen off a roof, with his hair all messed up and his bow tie crooked. He gripped a tennis racket like a baseball bat.

"Eleanor, this is an emergency! Is your father here?"

Just then Dad came up behind me, the newspaper tucked under his arm. "Ah, Mr. Worthington. I was just reading about the terrible earthquake in Verulia. Did you see the newspaper?"

"No, I didn't, but –"

"Fortunately, not many were hurt. But all the schools and hospitals collapsed, a lot of shops and houses were damaged, and even the playgrounds were wrecked. It's a real mess and there's no money to rebuild. My family visited Verulia, you know, although it is rather out of the way. Very picturesque mountain villages. A real tragedy."

"Well, I haven't come about any earthquake in some faraway land, Manfred. I've come about something happening right here."

"Have you been playing tennis, Mr. Worthington? I didn't know you were into sports. It's the new fitness craze, is it?"

"No, I haven't been playing tennis. I've been protecting my home and family. Listen to me, Manfred," he said, leaning over me to bring his face up to my dad's so that I was practically squeezed between them. "They've brought dinosaurs back to life. I don't know how. Maybe they've cloned them from fossils. Or created them in a laboratory. All I know is, one of those vicious winged dinosaurs . . ."

"A pterodactyl?" I offered.

"That's right, a pterodactyl. It tried to eat Mrs. Worthington. It swooped down out of the sky right at her. Why, if I hadn't fought it off, who knows what would have happened."

To demonstrate what he had done, Mr. Worthington whooshed the tennis racket over my head. Dad had to step back to avoid being smacked.

"Really?" said my father, crossing his arms. "By any chance, did this pterodactyl happen to be wearing green pajamas?"

"Well, it was green all right. The sun was in our eyes, but I could see the color. Green and horrible. A bloodthirsty carnivore. Why if I hadn't –"

He whooshed the racket through the air again, brushing the top of my hair and tapping Dad on the chin.

"Sorry, Manfred. Bit excited. We've got to do something. The next thing you know, there'll be a Tyrannosaurus rex running down the street. I'm going to call the police. Or maybe the air force. Maybe that's who I should call."

"I'm sure that isn't necessary. There must be some explanation. I just can't think of one."

Of course, I knew what it had been. Or rather, *who* it had been. My little brother, Solly. While I didn't want to defend him, I didn't want our secret getting out either. I had to think fast.

"I know what it was," I said.

"What?" said Dad and Mr. Worthington together.

"Solly's radio-controlled aeroplane. The one we just gave him for his birthday. He's been flying it too low. The other day, he knocked the cap right off the mailman's head."

"Yes, of course," Dad said, patting me on the shoulder. I could tell he was complimenting me for my quick thinking. "I'll have to give Solly a talk about airline safety procedures, won't I?"

"I don't see anything funny about it, Manfred. At this very moment, Mrs. Worthington is in the bathroom with a compress on her head and her feet in an ice bucket. She's very sensitive, and if I hadn't come along to . . . hey, wait a minute. Solly's birthday is in the winter. My Jeremy always gets invited to the party. So why does he have a new birthday present now?"

"That's a good question," Dad said. "And, uh, I'm sure Eleanor can answer that for us. Can't you, Eleanor?" His hand tapped my shoulder.

"Sure," I said. "It's on account of his pet rat."

"Pardon me?" said Mr. Worthington.

"You see," I went on, "Solly wanted to have the same birthday as G.W. That's what he named his rat, short for Googoo-whiskers. But G.W. was born in the spring. Solly didn't want to wait until his own birthday in February, so he decided to change the day. That's why he got his birthday present early."

"Yes," Dad said. "That's why."

"You let your son change his birthday?"

Dad looked embarrassed. "We're too indulgent, I know. But it meant a lot to him."

"To have the same birthday as a rat? Why does he even want to have the same birthday as a rat?"

"Well, that's quite obvious," my father said. "Tell him, Eleanor."

"So they can be twins. Twins have the same birthday, you see."

"That's true," Dad said. "Twins *do* have the same birthday."

"Well, if you want your son to be twins with a furry, skinny-tailed rodent, that's your business. But you just tell that rat – I mean, that boy – not to fly his aeroplane over our property."

"Don't worry about that," Dad said, "I'll tell him, all right."

2

THE ZOOMERS

After Mr. Worthington left, Dad called a conference in the family room. I knew what that meant. I tried to talk him out of it, but he was too annoyed to listen. He sent Solly and me to the sofa while he and Mom whispered in the hallway. Beside me, Solly crossed his legs and tried to look innocent.

"Nice weather we're having," he said.

I didn't answer.

"If it doesn't rain."

Nothing from me.

"You ever try to balance a piece of spaghetti on your nose?"

"I'm not talking to you," I said.

"But you just talked to me! Anyway, what did I do?"

"As if you don't know."

"Ha! You talked to me again."

Mom and Dad came in and stood before us. "That's it," Dad said. "You two are grounded. Flying during the day and letting people see you is a serious offense."

"That isn't fair," I said. "It's Solly who is always breaking the rules. I told him not to fly during the day, and not to scare Mrs. Worthington. Why do I have to be grounded too?"

"It's not just a punishment," Mom said. "The Worthingtons saw Solly. It's too risky to fly right now. Anyway, I think it would be good if both of you concentrate on schoolwork for a while. So, no flying until further notice."

"Thanks a lot, Googoo-man," I snarled under my breath. I was so mad at Solly, I could have pinched him. I was planning to fly tonight, after dark, and now I couldn't. I wanted to fly; I *needed* to fly! Lately I'd been feeling down about everything and flying just made me feel better. My mother said that at my age it's normal to be moody, but it felt pretty weird. And now I couldn't even fly.

So I did pinch Solly.

"Ow!" Solly jumped up from the sofa.

"Eleanor," Dad said, "keep your hands to yourself."

"Hey, what time is it?" Solly asked.

"Almost seven," said Mom. "Why?"

"Turn the TV on. Quick! It's time for *The Zoomers*."

"Do we have to watch it?" Dad said.

Dad was the only one who said he didn't like the show, but he watched it with us anyway. I don't think he really would have missed it. He even went over and turned on the TV. Mom had already made popcorn and we all settled down in our seats within grabbing distance of the big bowl. Solly had his rat, G.W., on his shoulder, and gave him a piece of popcorn. G.W. held it in his little paws as he ate. The commercial ended and the theme music to the show began. Over a picture of a house that looked a lot like ours, only it was about three times as big, came the words

THE ZOOMERS

They faded out, to be replaced by

WRITTEN, PRODUCED, AND DIRECTED
BY I.M. PARTANKISS

After that came

STARRING

A man jogged onto the screen in a tight-fitting superhero outfit, but without any mask. He scanned the horizon.

Rupert Musk as GEORGE ZOOMER

A woman in a matching superhero outfit jogged up beside him, her cape waving behind her. She, too, scanned the horizon and nodded.

Elizabeth Jenkens as LILY ZOOMER

Then the camera pulled back a little and two kids in superhero outfits ran up to their parents, who hugged them.

FEATURING Stevie Levine as GEORGE, JR.
and Amanda Devine as FRANCINE

Solly said, "How come it's only 'featuring' the kids, but it's 'starring' the grown-ups?"

"Shh," the rest of us said. Just then the picture faded to a view of a mist-covered mountain before switching to a dark laboratory inside it. Over a table of smoking and bubbling vials leaned a man in a black cape. He was completely bald and had a little tuft of hair under his lower lip. He looked up and straight into the camera, with a cruel glint in his eye, and stroked his mustache.

And Marvin Slouch as THE EVIL KARL SNOOP

Then the image of the evil Karl Snoop faded to blue sky. And flying in the sky were the mom, Lily Zoomer, and the kids, George, Jr. and Francine. They didn't really look like us flying; they had their arms stretched out and hands together, like they were diving, and they kicked their legs. In truth, they looked pretty dumb. Also, the sky behind them looked totally fake. Down on the street below was the dad, George Zoomer, riding a motor scooter.

"Hey!" George shouted, as he did every week. "Wait for me!"

Dad said, "I hate it when he says that."

The new episode began. In it, the evil Karl Snoop had devised a secret formula in his laboratory deep inside Misery Mountain. He planned to sneak the formula into all the factories around the world that made bubble gum. The formula would affect the bubble gum so that it wouldn't stretch and you couldn't blow bubbles. Of course, the Zoomers found out about it, snuck into the lab in Misery Mountain, and destroyed the formula. Karl Snoop got away (he jumped onto the back of a passing subway train), and the Zoomers all got medals from the mayor.

"Thank you, Zoomer-man and Zoomer-woman. Thank you, Zoomer-boy and Zoomer-girl," said the mayor, while newspaper photographers snapped their pictures.

To be honest, it wasn't much different from last week's episode, when Karl Snoop invented a machine that turned all crayons gray, so that kids wouldn't be able to draw sunsets and rainbows and anything else in color. Or the week before that, when he invented a kind of giant vacuum cleaner that sucked up music, so there would be no pop music, no rock or rap or any other kind. Every time, the Zoomers managed to defeat Karl Snoop, and every time, Karl Snoop got away.

So it wasn't for the stories that I liked *The Zoomers*. It was because, even though the millions of people who watched it just thought it was made up, the show was really based on us. Of course, there were differences. For one thing, unlike me and Solly, the kids never argued. And their parents were never mad at them. They had great rooms, with their own computers and stereos, and bunk beds with real slides down to the floor. As superheroes, they were famous and everybody loved them. Karl Snoop was evil, but he was also hard to take seriously – unlike the real Kaspar Snit. The show never explained the secret of how the Zoomers could fly. They would talk about "the secret" in whispers, but they never explained it. There was a pretty simple reason for that.

At first we couldn't understand how someone could make a television show that seemed to be about our family and how we had defeated Kaspar Snit. *Was it a coincidence? Did somebody know about us?* But then, one night we were watching the show and, during the commercials, I doodled on the edge of the newspaper. I wrote out "Partankiss" and then, just for fun, started mixing the letters around.

Karpantiss.

Kasparnits.

Kasparsnit.

Kaspar Snit.

Kaspar Snit! I was so shocked that I couldn't speak for a moment. When I could talk again, I said, "Mom, Dad, you won't believe it!"

"*Shh!*" Solly said. "The show's on."

"But I have to tell you something."

"Wait until the next commercial, dear," Mom said.

And so I had to wait. Finally the commercial came on and Dad said, "All right, Eleanor, what's so important?"

"Oh, nothing," I shrugged. "Just that I.M. Partankiss is actually Kaspar Snit."

"*What?*"

That sure got their attention. Of course, even with the name we couldn't be sure, but the next day Dad found a picture of I.M. Partankiss on the cover of *Famous People* magazine. It was Kaspar Snit all right. He looked a little different, with cool black sunglasses and his hair slicked back and a French beret on his head, but it was him. We didn't know how Kaspar Snit, who had escaped months ago from an Italian jail, ended up with his own show. But now we watched it every week.

The closing credits came on. "Well," Mom said, "I think it's heartening that a person can turn his life around. Kaspar Snit was a very bad man, trying to steal the fountains of Rome. And now look at him. He's a successful television producer. Kids love his show. It just proves that you should never lose faith in somebody."

"Yes," Dad said, "but why does he have to make the father act so foolishly? The way he rides around on that little motor scooter, beeping his horn! At least he could have a real motorcycle."

"What I don't get," Solly said, "is why nobody figures

out that the Zoomers are superheroes. They don't even wear masks. And they use their real name."

The commercial ended. *"Stay tuned,"* said the announcer, *"for our next show,* Behind the Scenes, *and an exclusive interview with the creator of the hit show* The Zoomers, *I.M. Partankiss."*

"Oh, let's watch," Mom said. "I'd like to hear what he has to say."

"Me, too," I said. And I meant it; I was eager to see Kaspar Snit after all these months. I didn't necessarily want to be in the same room with him, but seeing him on TV would be all right.

The show came on and a woman with puffy hair was standing in front of an iron gate with the words PARTANKISS PRODUCTIONS over it.

– *Good evening and welcome to* Behind the Scenes, *where you get to peek into the magic of television. Tonight we are going inside Partankiss Productions to speak to I.M. Partankiss, the genius behind your favorite show,* The Zoomers. *As you can see behind me, Partankiss Productions works out of an unusual space, a former amusement park that used to be called Conlin's.*

"Hey," Solly said, "that's near us!"

– *In fact, the studios where the shows are filmed can be found inside the artificial mountain that rises in the center of the old amusement park. It used to be called*

Fun Mountain, but, as you fans know, on the show it's the hideout of Karl Snoop, who calls it Misery Mountain. Now come with me to meet none other than I.M. Partankiss.

The camera switched and now we saw the woman with the puffy hair opposite I.M. Partankiss. They were sitting in front of the set for the Zoomers' house. "Oh, my!" said my mom. It was Kaspar Snit all right, with his hair and his sunglasses and his beret, only now he wore a black velvet cape studded with sparkling diamonds. He still had his pointed black beard, but now his long mustache was curled into loops. He was smiling, his extra-white teeth ("He must have had them bleached," Dad said) showing.

– Mr. Partankiss, it's an honor to meet you.

– Of course it is.

– May I call you I.M.?

– No, you may not.

– All right, then. Please tell us, how did you come up with the idea for The Zoomers*? I mean, it's brilliant. A family that can fly, except for the father. An evil genius. Where does it all come from?*

– Ah, who knows where creativity comes from? It's something of a mystery. A gift, even. You either have it or you don't. I suppose I'm just a remarkably special person.

– You certainly are. But there must have been some influences.

– Of course. No artist works in a vacuum. I was influenced by a number of great works of literature. Peter Pan. The Wizard of Oz. *But when you come down to it, my show is unique and, in all modesty, far superior to anything that has come before it.*

– And why do you think your show is so popular?

– Because people want to believe in something. Sure, maybe in real life flying is just a fantasy. But we can dream, can't we? And if we dream, who knows what we can achieve. I think that my show gives kids and adults everywhere something to dream about. And hope. Hoping and dreaming, that's what it's about.

– What a beautiful message.

– Yes, it is. After all, I came up with it. And, of course, the show is masterfully written, produced, and directed, also by me. Now I really must get back to work. But if I might mention something. . . .

– Of course.

Kaspar Snit reached behind his chair and pulled out a plastic figure, a girl in a superhero outfit. He pressed a button – the arms swung forward and the legs started to kick. Kaspar Snit looked right into the camera and smiled.

– Here they are, children, just what you've been waiting for. Zoomer dolls! And you can buy the Zoomer family house, the motor scooter, and many other expensive accessories. Batteries not included. So hurry to your local toy store. And remember, when you're in town, take a tour of the Partankiss Productions' studio. Tickets are very reasonable!

– Thank you, I.M. Partankiss, for giving us some of your precious time.

– Yes, generous of me, wasn't it?

Dad got up and turned off the television.

Solly picked G.W. off his shoulder. The rat twitched his whiskers. Solly made him swoop through the air. "I want a Zoomer doll! I want Zoomer-boy. I want all of them!"

I was older than Solly and knew better than to just blurt out that I wanted something. Parents never rush out and buy you a new toy just because you demand it. But I felt the same as Solly. I wanted a Zoomer-girl doll, and I wanted her clothes and all her other accessories too.

3

ROMANCE STINKS

Solly went to bed earlier than me, something he always complained about. He also complained that I got a bigger allowance, that I was allowed to walk to school by myself, and about everything else I got to do because I was older. The girl on *The Zoomers* never had to listen to her brother whine. She was prettier than me too, with a little turned-up nose and perfect hair. And she never, ever got grounded. Television was definitely better than life.

At Solly's bedtime, Mom and Dad called me in for a family chat. Solly was playing with G.W., letting the rat investigate the top of his dresser. Mom and Dad decided that a pet would be good for Solly, who didn't have a lot of friends to play with since Ginger Hirshbein moved with his family to Cow Head, Newfoundland. G.W. was a hooded rat, which meant that he was mostly white but with a toffee-colored head and a little stripe down his back. He was pretty cute, with his little ears and whiskers and bright eyes and soft fur. He was smart and he was friendly, always wanting to play, sneaking into pockets to look for cookie crumbs.

"Solly," Mom said, "say good night to G.W. and come to bed. And don't kiss him on the nose."

"Okay, Mom," Solly said, kissing G.W. on the nose. Then he gave G.W. a rat treat and put him in his cage, before jumping into bed. Dad came in, too, and turned out the light so that there was only the glow of the night-light underneath Solly's bed. Even Googoo-man could be a little afraid of the dark.

"Dad," I said, as my parents sat on the edge of Solly's bed. "Was there really an earthquake in Verulia?"

"Uh-huh. It's in the paper. In fact, there's a picture of Kaspar Snit's old fortress on the top of Mount Darkling. Or what *was* his old fortress. The government was going to turn it into a tourist attraction, but it's a bunch of rubble now."

"Hey," Solly said, "I wonder what happened to the captain of Kaspar Snit's army. You remember, the one who wanted to be a ballet dancer. He would have been a good guide for the fortress tour."

"I think the fortress is the last thing they must be worried about in Verulia," Mom said. "Schools and hospitals come before tourist attractions."

"I could see hospitals," said Solly. "But schools?"

"I have another question," I said. "How come we don't turn Kaspar Snit in? I mean, he broke out of jail, didn't he?"

"That's a good question," Dad said. "Mom and I have thought about it. And, strictly speaking, you're right. We ought to tell the authorities where Kaspar Snit is. But then he'd go back to jail."

"And maybe that would be a shame, considering that he's reformed himself," Mom said. "He's not doing evil anymore and we just haven't had the heart to do it. At least, I haven't."

"He did steal those fountains," Dad said. "He caused a lot of trouble. Sometimes I do think he ought to pay for it. And did you hear him in that interview, Daisy? Maybe he's reformed, but he's still awfully full of himself."

"How can he be full of himself?" Solly asked. "Unless he ate himself."

"It means he brags a lot," Mom said. "Which, indeed, he does. But this is not why we're sitting here, is it, Manfred? We wanted to tell you kids something. It's just a little thing, nothing to get upset about. Manfred, you tell them."

"I knew you'd chicken out," Dad said. "Okay. You know how Mom and I sometimes talk about how we don't get any time together? You know, alone, as a couple."

"You mean, *romantic* time?" Solly said, fluttering his eyes.

"Well, yes. So your mom and I decided that, after more than twelve years, it's time for us to take a holiday together. So next Sunday morning, we're going to Italy."

"Hurray – we're going to Italy!" Solly cried, jumping up and down on the bed.

"No, darling," Mom said gently. "Just your dad and me. You and Eleanor are staying home. After all, you do have school."

"That's such a rip-off," Solly said. "You don't love us."

"Of course we do," Dad said.

"Then can we go?"

"No, Solly."

I didn't say anything, but I was as disappointed as Solly. *My parents take a vacation without us? Why would they want to do that?* It couldn't possibly be any fun. And I didn't want to be left behind. *Romance*, I thought, *stinks*.

"You can't leave us alone," I said. "I don't know how to cook. And I can't drive the car. . . ."

"Of course not," Dad said, putting his hand on mine. "You both need someone to take care of you. And that's why we've gone to the very best agency to hire a nanny for the two weeks."

"A nanny?" Solly said. "We've never had a nanny before. What's her name?"

"Mrs. Leer," said Mom. "I'm sure you're going to like her."

"Have you met her?" I asked.

"No, but I spoke to her on the phone and told her all about you two. Except about flying, of course. That's a secret."

"Is she bringing Mr. Leer with her?" Solly asked.

"I'm afraid that she's a widow."

"She's a *window*?" Solly said.

"No, a widow," I said. "That means her husband kicked the bucket."

"He knocked over a pail?"

Mom sighed. "No, Solly. He died."

"Did she poison him?" Solly asked.

"Of course not. Where do you get such ideas? Now I expect you two to be cooperative. I want a good report when we get home."

"Can we fly while you're away?" I asked.

"We'll think about it," Dad said.

The night wasn't perfect for flying. It was warm and humid, which meant the possibility of sudden updrafts and maybe rain. And the sky was black and starless, which meant that I couldn't see the North Star or any others that might help me navigate my way home again. But I decided to go anyway, even though we were grounded.

Or maybe *because* we were grounded. That was something new in me, along with what Mom called my moods. I didn't always want to be good, so that Mom and Dad would compliment me and tell me how great I was. Sometimes I wanted to be, well, a little bad. Just to see what it felt like. Or maybe just to make more choices for myself.

It was almost midnight. I was standing in the living room with the window open, feeling the warm air on my face. I looked at my hand to see how much of the markings were left from the last imprint I had made from my mother's ancient amulet. I could see the quarter moon and the three stars – faint purple markings on my palm – but they had faded. I had maybe a couple of days of flying left. The odd thing was, lately some of the markings – a thin outline of the three stars and the moon – had been very slow to fade. The last couple of times, they hadn't even faded completely. I'd been left with the outline of two stars and half the moon.

I put my arms at my sides, tilted my hands at a thirty-degree angle, closed my eyes, and rose up on my toes. I tried to clear my mind of everything and, a moment later, I could feel my body move silently up through the open window and into the night.

When I opened my eyes, I was hovering above the roof of our house. Then I began to fly north, over the crescents and streets, the Rooster's Fried Chicken, the hockey arena, the water tower. It was hard to believe my parents were really going away without us. Why couldn't they just leave Solly with a nanny, so that I could go with them? Mrs. Leer was probably some horrible old witch who hated kids, drank whiskey, clipped her toenails over the kitchen sink, and smoked long smelly cigars. I ought to do something to register my protest. I could go on a hunger strike. I could run away.

Or I could go and visit Kaspar Snit.

It had been almost a year since I'd learned the secret of how my mother could fly. And since Kaspar Snit had stolen all the fountains of Rome, and our fountain too, so that we had to fly all the way to his fortress in Verulia to get them back. By now, flying seemed so natural that it felt as if I'd always been able to do it. I didn't let three days go by without taking a little trip and, at least once a month, Mom, Solly, and I would fly somewhere new – up to Hudson's Bay, over Chicago, along the Adirondack Mountains. Solly always dressed as Googoo-man, but I didn't need a cape or goggles to feel like I was a super-anything. Just flying made me feel that way. Of course, Dad didn't come with us since he couldn't fly, but he claimed not to mind. He would stay home and play his mandolin, or work on his latest project to restore an ancient fountain in Madrid or build a new one in St. Petersburg. Still, Mom didn't like to leave him too often.

As for Kaspar Snit, sometimes he seemed like someone who had appeared in one of my bad dreams, someone who wasn't actually real. But at other times I would remember the chilling sound of his voice, or how he would ask me to join him in a life of evildoing and then grow furious when I refused. I would remember how much he hated not only me, but Solly, Mom, and Dad too.

But I had thought about him less and less, at least until *The Zoomers* went on the air and I figured out who I.M. Partankiss was. Mom and Dad said that we didn't have anything to worry about anymore, now that he was a television big shot. "He makes lots of money," Dad said, "and he even gets to be famous. Just what Kaspar Snit has always wanted. He's realized that he doesn't have to be evil. He just has to have a television show."

I figured that Dad was right, but every so often I still thought about Kaspar Snit and felt a shiver go through me. Now, as I flew through the dark, I could see the old Conlin's Amusement Park below. The Ferris wheel was still there, and the roller coaster, although I could see they were shut down. A light shone on Misery Mountain, as it was now called. Another light shone on the front gate and, dropping lower, I could make out the new words in wrought iron. PARTANKISS PRODUCTIONS. I bet Kaspar Snit would be surprised if I knocked on the door to say hello. The only thing was, I didn't have the nerve to do it. Not by myself, in the dark. Anyway, he probably wasn't there at night.

Instead, I made a wide-banking turn and headed home. There was a breeze at my back to help me along and I soared upwards and then swooped down again, moving through the air with ease. It was like windsurfing through the sky. In pretty good time, I could see our house below. It was easy to spot, with the fountain filling up our whole front garden. Out of the middle rose eight marble horses, rearing up on their hind legs, and eight full-size men and women, each without a stitch of clothing, holding up conch shells. Now that the neighbors had decided they liked the fountain, Dad kept some small colored spotlights on it. During the day water spurted from the shells, but at night he turned the water off so that the sound of splashing wouldn't disturb people.

Gently coming down, I felt so different from when I had taken off. Fresh and calm and content. Closing my eyes, I slipped through the window and felt my bare feet touch the carpet. And then I heard something.

"Ahem."

I opened my eyes and saw Dad, Mom, and Solly looking at me. They all had their arms crossed and wore scowls. Even G.W., on Solly's shoulder, looked mad at me. Deciding on my defense, I blinked and yawned, as if I had just been asleep.

"Oh, gee. What's going on? Why aren't I in bed? I must have been walking in my sleep."

"Try flying in your sleep," Solly said.

"Hey, you're the one who got us grounded."

"All right, that's enough, you two," Mom said. "Eleanor, you knew that you weren't supposed to fly tonight. What kind of an example are you setting for your younger brother by breaking the rules?"

"I don't want to be an example."

"I just don't know what's gotten into you," Mom said. "Manfred?"

My dad shrugged. "There is definitely going to be no flying while your mom and I are away. We can't trust either of you to be responsible."

"Oh, give her a break, Dad," Solly said. "She's a preteen. You know how crazy they are. Their brains are all mixed up. It's a scientific fact. Scientists have studied them in laboratories."

"You're making that up," I said.

"I really do need a holiday," Mom groaned. "And Dad's right. There's going to be no flying. Now, everyone march right back to bed."

"Can I have an ice-cream sundae?" Solly asked.

"In the middle of the night? Of course not."

We walked back down the hall. "An ice-cream sundae?" I whispered. "Did you really think Mom would say yes?"

"I figured it was one in a million," he whispered back. "But that means if I ask a million times, one time she's going to say yes."

"A million is a lot of times to ask."

"I know. I've got nine hundred and ninety-nine thousand, nine hundred and ninety-nine to go."

Dad took Solly back to his room and Mom took me to mine. Solly would probably dream about ice-cream sundaes. And I was going to dream about flying. Or, rather, *not* flying.

4

SCRUB, SCRUB, SCRUB

The next Saturday morning I wanted to sleep in, but there was so much noise in the house that even putting a pillow over my ears didn't help. The crashing of tin buckets, the bellow of my father singing Italian opera out of tune, not to mention the pounding on my door, all forced me to get up and dress.

I had forgotten. Today was fountain-cleaning day.

We had a fountain-cleaning day every three months. That was when we had to bring out stiff brushes, mops, old sheets cut up into rags, and buckets of soapy water to scrub the fountain clean of dirt and grime and spots of green algae, so that once again the marble shone, as my dad put it, "like a sculpture by Michelangelo." It was a big job, with that giant basin, the eight full-sized horses and riders, and we all had to help. But my dad led the charge.

Mom had prepared pancakes to stoke up our energy. After we ate, we headed outside, where there was already a line of kids and teenagers along the sidewalk to watch. I saw that Solly had made a booth out of a big cardboard box and had painted a sign.

FOUNTAIN-CLEANING TICKETS

FRONT ROW – 25 CENTS
BACK ROW – 15 CENTS

POPCORN – 15 CENTS

YELLING FUNNY COMMENTS – FREE!

He wore his baseball cap backwards and was collecting the money in a tin can. The popcorn was from a bowl in the kitchen, left over from three days ago. "Good places, going fast!" Solly shouted, like a hot-dog seller at the ball game. "Get 'em while you can." But when Mom saw what Solly was up to, she made him give the money back and go in the house to change and help.

I wore rubber boots, old jeans, and a T-shirt, and it wasn't long before I was soaking wet and covered in soap bubbles. While I used a brush to scrub the legs of the horses, Dad, up on a ladder, cleaned the figures. He kept dumping soapy water on the rest of us. Mom worked inside the basin, where the most algae had grown. Solly came out of the house wearing a bathing suit, swim mask, snorkel, and carrying a toy spear-gun. Some help he was.

"Scrub, everybody!" Dad called, from high up on the ladder. "Put some muscle into it! Let's get this fountain shining! Hey, Eleanor, you want to come up and help clean the figures?"

Scrub a marble butt? No thank you. "I'm kind of busy down here," I said. I brushed a soapy strand of hair from my eyes and looked over at the sidewalk. Just then the Worthingtons pulled up in their car and Julia and Jeremy stood by the open back door with big bags in their hands. They joined the crowd on the sidewalk to watch. *Oh, great.* The last thing I needed was for Julia Worthington to see me looking like this.

"Hey, Eleanor," Julia said, "you missed a spot."

I considered squeezing my soapy sponge over her shoes, but decided to look as if I was having fun instead. Solly pushed up his swim mask. "What have you got in those bags?" he said. It was always a mistake to ask Julia and Jeremy a question like that, but Solly couldn't resist.

"We went to Toy Heaven this morning," Jeremy said. "And guess what we got? Zoomer dolls!"

He reached into the bag and pulled out a box. Through the cellophane window, I could see the George, Jr. doll, positioned as if it were flying.

"Hey, that's me!" said Solly.

"In your dreams," Jeremy said.

"And we got Zoomer-man, Zoomer-woman, and Zoomer-girl too. And the house. And the motor scooter.

And Misery Mountain, with the working laboratory," Julia said.

"We spent two hundred and seventy-three dollars!" said Jeremy. "Come on, Julia, let's go inside and set them up."

Solly and I stood watching as they ran inside. We didn't even look at each other. We just returned to our scrubbing.

Back in my room and in dry clothes, I sat on my bed, playing my electric guitar. Or, at least, I played the three chords that I knew. Because my parents had bought Solly a rat, they let me get the guitar, and I'd been pretty enthusiastic for almost a whole month. But learning an instrument was hard and somehow I didn't get around to practising, so all I knew were the three chords I'd learned at the beginning. I still liked to play them, usually with the distortion button pressed on my little practise amp, to get a cool, thrashy sound. I still planned to learn and become a really great guitar player, but for the moment I mostly just pretended.

"Hey, Eleanor," Solly said, bursting through the doorway.

"You're supposed to knock!"

"I forgot."

He was wearing his full Googoo-man outfit – green pajamas, red bathing suit, bathing cap, goggles, towel with PROPERTY OF HOTEL SCHMUTZ on it. He'd traded in the flippers that he used to wear for a pair of those shoes with retractable skate wheels in them. He said that they were better for making a fast getaway. And he had two new weapons to replace his old ones, an electromagnetic scrambler, which looked exactly like his old bicycle horn, and a force-field generator, which looked remarkably like a box of baking powder dangling from a string.

"What do you want?" I said. "I thought you were mad at me for getting us grounded while Mom and Dad are away."

"I'm taking a time-out from being mad. I want you to hear my new Googoo-man song."

"Your what?"

Solly huffed in exasperation. "Every superhero has a song. Like the Zoomers on their show. I could hear Jeremy and Julia playing in their backyard. When you press a button on the house, the song comes out. So now I've got my own song."

"Okay, so sing it."

"You have to ask me nicely."

"Are you kidding me?"

"Never mind. But you have to stand up and listen. Out of respect."

"It's not a national anthem. All right, don't give me that dopey look. I'll stand up."

"Good."

Solly himself stood ramrod straight, tilted up his chin, and started to sing.

When you're in trouble, what do you do?
Call for the guy whose name is Goo!
He'll save the day, he'll stop the crime,
And he won't even charge a single dime.

Who's funny, who's cute,
Who's got strength, style, and speed?
Who doesn't cry when he gets a nosebleed?
Who can surf, bake a pie, drive a truck, make his bed?
Read all of *Harry Potter* while standing on his head?
You know his name, say it loud –
Googoo-man, Gogoo-man, you make us proud!

"So?" Solly said. "What do you think?"

I said, "You don't know how to surf. Or bake a pie. Or drive a truck."

"That's what's called poetic license. Mom told me."

"Poetic license means you can lie?"

"Exactly."

I thought for a moment. "It's perfect," I said.

Solly smiled and ran out of the room, shouting, "Dad, Dad! You have to hear my song!" One thing I had to say about Solly: it wasn't hard to make him happy.

I was supposed to spend some time after dinner working on my science project on the history of flight. My project was about the first aeroplanes that actually flew, like the Wright Brothers' *Kitty Hawk* that was built in 1903, but all I was doing was looking at pictures of flying machines that *didn't* work – motorcars with flapping wings attached, bicycles with a dozen propellers that spun when you pedaled. People desperate to fly had come up with some pretty crazy ideas, but I couldn't blame them since I was feeling pretty desperate myself.

I lay down on my bed, staring up at the ceiling. I decided that staring up at the ceiling was about the most boring thing I could do. But it seemed that I spent a lot of time this way lately, hanging around in my room, not doing much. I thought about my parents leaving for their holiday in the morning, but that only made me feel lonely. I decided to do something.

I scratched my nose.

There, now I could do nothing again. Taking my hand away from my face, I noticed the markings on my palm and decided to examine them. They had faded to a faint pink, except for the pencil-thin outline of two of the stars and about half the moon, which were a deep violet. It looked like, this time, more of the outline was staying behind. Overall, the markings were just visible enough to fly, although they could fade out anytime now. Even if I could have snuck outside, it wouldn't have been safe; if they suddenly disappeared, I might plunge out of the sky. But what about in my room? What about from a lying-down position? I'd never tried that before. Well, there was a first time for everything.

I closed my eyes, my head on the pillow. Cleared my mind. Positioned my hands, which lay on the quilt, at the proper angle. Maybe I wouldn't fly; maybe I would just fall asleep.

Ouch!

I opened my eyes. My nose had hit the ceiling! I was hovering in a horizontal position at the very top of my room. *Fantastic!* But I must have made a loud thump because suddenly there came a knock on my door.

"Eleanor?" Dad's voice. "Are you all right?"

The fright caused me to come down – *whomp!* – onto my bed.

The door opened. "Eleanor?" said Dad. "What's going on?"

"Oh, nothing," I said. "I was . . . I was just nailing up a picture."

"You've never been very good at fibbing, at least not to me. I know what you've been doing."

"You do?"

"You've been jumping on the bed. You're going to break it."

"I won't do it again."

"Okay."

"Hurry up, everybody!" It was Solly's voice. I could tell he was running up and down the hallway, like a toy electric car that wouldn't turn off. "*The Zoomers* is on in two minutes!"

Something to look forward to at last. I went to the living room to see that Mom had made the popcorn while Solly was skating around in his Googoo-man outfit, singing his new theme song.

I sat on the sofa beside Dad. "I really don't know why we even watch this show," he said. "The stories are corny. The actors are wooden. And the special effects are cheesy."

"Because we like it," Solly said. "And now Googoo-man will use his force-field generator to turn on the television." He pointed the weapon from his belt.

"How about we try the remote?" I said, pressing a button. But what came on the screen wasn't the opening of the show. Instead, we saw the gate of Partankiss Productions, with Misery Mountain in the background. Standing in front of the gate was the woman reporter with the puffy hair. She was holding a microphone and staring grimly into the camera.

– *Good evening, fans of* The Zoomers. *I have some disappointing news. The show is not available tonight. The television network is unsure why, but the writer, producer, and director of* The Zoomers, *I.M. Partankiss, is going to come out and tell us what the problem is. And here he is now. . . .*

From somewhere at the side, Kaspar Snit stepped into sight of the camera. Just like before, he wore sunglasses, a beret, and his diamond-encrusted cape. He looked straight into the camera, with a dark glint in his eye.

– *Mr. Partankiss, millions of viewers have been looking forward to the latest episode of* The Zoomers. *They want to know why it isn't going to be shown. Please tell us.*

– *Don't stick that microphone in my face! Yes, I'll tell all of you. The reason is, we are holding a fundraiser.*

– *A fundraiser?*

– That's right. We've been very fortunate with our success, and now the actors and I think it's time to do something for somebody else. As some of you fans know, the country of Verulia has been hit with a terrible catastrophe.

– Oh, yes, it's been on the news. An awful earthquake.

– I happen to have a great fondness for Verulia. You might say that I spent some of my best years there. So we on The Zoomers *have decided to raise money for all those unlucky Verulians. The actors and I are going to donate a week's salary to the special Help Verulia Fund that I have just established. And I would like all you fans to send in your donations too. Send your dollars, your quarters, your nickels, and your pennies. Send in your lunch money and your allowance. Every penny will help. Just send it to the address on this card.* The Zoomers *show will go back on the air when we have raised one million dollars. I will deliver it personally to the people of Verulia.*

– Why, that's amazing, Mr. Partankiss. It is so generous, so public-spirited. This hardened reporter must admit to having a tear in her eye. You heard it here, fans. If you want your favorite show back, then send in your donations. Here, Mr. Partankiss, take everything in my wallet.

– How good of you. What, only seven dollars? Well, it's a start. I'm sure our fans will respond to this cry for assistance. Help Verulia today!

– Well, fans, there you have it. Please stay tuned for a rerun of last year's semifinal lacrosse game between Sweden and Brazil.

The image flickered out and in its place was a green sports field, with men in shorts running about with funny sticks. Dad got up and turned off the television. "Well, I never would have expected it," he said.

"He really is a new man," Mom said. "I'm very impressed."

"Well, Googoo-man is going to do something about it," Solly said.

"What?" I asked.

"Send money, of course. I've got two dollars saved up."

"That's very generous of you," Mom said, putting her arm around him. "And we'll add a hundred. Well, your father and I have to finish packing. It's a big day tomorrow for all of us."

No *Zoomers*. Dad was right – it wasn't a very good show. But I was still disappointed. Now all I had to think about was Mom and Dad leaving in the morning. And there wasn't any fun in that.

5 THE WIDOW LEER

The morning newspaper had an article in the entertainment section about *The Zoomers*. There was a picture of a smiling I.M. Partankiss, light glinting on his teeth, holding up the card with the address for sending in donations. According to the article, which Dad read aloud to us, a hundred envelopes arrived by special delivery within an hour of last night's broadcast. I.M. Partankiss said that it warmed his heart to see the fans sending in their nickels and dimes to help people who lived so far away. He would get the money to the earthquake victims as soon as it reached a million dollars.

"At this rate," Dad said, "you should have your television show back in no time."

"Tell you what, Dad," I said. "How about instead of going to Italy this morning, you stick around and see when it comes back on?"

Dad just patted me on the head. My parents' suitcases and knapsacks were already packed and waiting at the front door. Their taxicab was supposed to arrive not long after the nanny. Mom said, "Now, kids, I want you to give Mrs. Leer a real family welcome when she arrives."

"You mean like this?" Solly said. He stuck his fingers into his ears, stuck out his tongue, and made a loud noise: *"BTTHHHHHAAA!"*

"Don't you dare," Dad said.

But Solly, I noticed, had dressed in full Googoo-man outfit to meet her and had even polished his goggles. When I looked away and out the front window, I saw a woman standing on the sidewalk beside a small car with a trunk strapped to the roof. She was very tall, with gangly arms and rather large feet. She wore her bird's nest of hair pinned up, and a khaki skirt and one of those vests with a million pockets for going camping or mountain climbing. She was staring up at our fountain.

"Mom, Dad, I think you better take a look," I said.

"What is it?" Mom asked, coming over. I saw the expression on her face change to dismay. "Manfred," she said, "did we tell Mrs. Leer about the fountain?"

"Why, did we need to?" Dad stopped talking. He had spotted her staring at the fountain too.

"We should have warned her, Manfred. Do something before she gets in the car and drives away."

"Right," Dad said, but before he could move, we saw the woman marching up the walkway to our door. All of us rushed to the front hall, but Dad got there first and opened the door just as she arrived.

"Mrs. Leer," Dad said, in a falsely cheerful voice. "No doubt you've noticed our little ornament on the lawn. Perhaps you are surprised, or even a little, well, shocked, as our neighbors were at first. But if you take a moment to consider the history of western art –"

"No need, no need!" cried Mrs. Leer. "I took one look at it and the civilizations of ancient Greece and Rome rose before me. It is magnificent. A celebration of the human spirit."

"And the horse spirit," said Solly.

"Yes, quite, young man. In short, I adore it."

"That is a relief," said Mom.

"It so happens," Mrs. Leer went on, "that the second man on the left reminds me of my late husband, the dear, dreary Mr. Leer, as I always called him with affection. Of course, Mr. Leer wasn't so muscular, nor so tall, nor so slim. And his nose was rather more bulbous. But otherwise, it is the spitting image of him."

"It must be very difficult for you," Dad said.

"Yes, very."

"Was it recent – his passing?" asked my mother.

"Twelve years. Twelve years, six months, and three days. Ate a bad oyster. I told him it looked off, looked as if it was winking at me. But he loved his shellfish. He was from Brighton, you see. Of course, he was much older than I was. Well, I had a good life before, and I'm having a good life after, and that's the sum of it. And if I might speak the truth, I am absolutely parched for a cup of tea."

"Of course," Mom said. "Perhaps we better just bring in your trunk."

"If the juniors would help me, I'd be much obliged. I think it does children good to pitch in. You must be Eleanor," she said, looking me in the eyes with a kindly smile. "Never Ellen or Elly."

"That's right," I said, not being able to hold back my own smile.

"And you," she said again, this time turning to Solly, "are the world's youngest superhero. I believe your talents will come in very handy over the next two weeks."

"At your service, ma'am," Solly said, standing at attention.

"But where is your little pointy-nosed assistant? G.W. by name, I believe."

"Here. I sewed a pocket in my cape, see? He likes it in there."

"So he does. He's poking his head out to say hello. I'll just give him a scratch behind the ears. That's it. But listen, you two, if you think helping me with that trunk means that the two weeks are going to be work, work, work, then you are mistaken. I'm afraid I have to tell you that I am a nanny who believes that homework, dishes, and the like must be relieved with liberal amounts of play time. If you want a taskmaster, then you have hired the wrong nanny."

"No!" Solly and I said together.

"Right. Then off we go to the Leermobile!"

The trunk was covered with stickers from just about everywhere in the world – Brazil, Finland, Egypt, Nepal, New Zealand. Mrs. Leer carried one end by herself; being so tall, she had to bend over to keep her end from rising much higher than ours. After we brought it in, we all sat down in the kitchen for tea. Dad brought the pot to the table and Mom the teacups, along with a plate of cookies.

Solly said, "You don't seem like most nannies."

Mrs. Leer took a slurp of tea. "Well, Solly, perhaps those others are not card-carrying members of the I.U.E.C."

"What's the I.U.E.C.?"

"The International Union of Extraordinary Caregivers. We are, if I may sound immodest, a select group. Our standards are the very highest. Now, Mr. Blande and Ms. Galinski, if I might ask, what part of Italy are you visiting?"

"Tuscany," said my father.

"Ah, Tuscany! It was dear, dreary Mr. Lear's favorite place. Ideal for romance renewed. Meanwhile, your progeny will be well tended. Fed and watered at regular intervals. Given nine-and-a-half hours' sleep. Mental and physical stimulations of the most healthful kind. Occasional infusions of ice cream and chocolate. And now I see by my official I.U.E.C. watch that your taxi should arrive in thirty seconds. If it does not, we shall telephone the company and demand to know what sort of fly-by-night operation they are running."

The doorbell rang.

"Very good. Children, it is time to wish your parents a bon voyage. Kiss them good-bye, wave farewell, and be done with it!"

While Mrs. Leer insisted on carrying out the luggage, we said good-bye to our parents. First Dad hugged me tight and said into my ear, "Have fun, sweetie pie. Be good, but not too good. And keep an eye on Solly. You know the mischief he can get into."

"I will," I mumbled into his shoulder.

Next came Mom. "I'll miss you awfully," she said. "You watch out for your brother, will you? He does get into trouble sometimes."

"I will."

"All loaded up," reported a breathless Mrs. Leer as she returned to the porch. "I've instructed the driver to open the windows and to keep within the speed limit."

"Thank you," Mom said. "Oh, I almost forgot." She reached into her shirt and pulled out a thin chain. On the end of the chain dangled the ancient silver amulet. The sun reflected from it as it turned.

"How lovely," Mrs. Leer said.

"Would you mind taking care of it while we're gone? It's a family heirloom. I wouldn't want it to get lost."

"Have no fear," Mrs. Leer said, taking it from my mother. She tucked it into one of the pockets on her vest and did up the zipper. "It's as safe as if it were in the bank.

Now be off before you are late. Partings are always difficult. Generations torn asunder. Futures unknown. But there is always the sweet reunion to look forward to. And as for you two, I have a new recipe for upside-down pineapple fudge cake. Who wants to help?"

Mrs. Leer was going to use my parents' bedroom for her own while they were away. We hauled the trunk along the hallway and into the room, and Mrs. Leer undid the clasps and opened it up.

"I smell apple pie!" said Solly.

"And vanilla ice cream!" I added.

"You have excellent noses. That is my favorite perfume. As a result, I am very popular with children and dogs. Your parents were kind enough to empty these drawers for me. I shall put my knickers in here."

She took out blouses, shawls, skirts, a kit with a toothbrush, and other bathroom things. "There are only three items left in this trunk," she said. "My most valuable possessions." The first was a small picture frame. In it was an old photograph of a man with round eyes, a balding head, and a tiny mustache. He was smiling very pleasantly.

"Is that the dear, dreary Mr. Leer?" I asked.

"Indeed," sighed Mrs. Leer.

"He looks kind of puny," said Solly.

"Solly!"

"That's all right," Mrs. Leer said. "In fact, he was not a big man. I would lift him up easily in moments of exuberant affection. He enjoyed it, except in the presence of company. As always, I shall place him on the night table beside my pillow."

She did so, turning the frame one way and then another, until she was satisfied. Then she unzipped one of her vest pockets and took out the amulet. She draped the chain over the picture frame.

"What about the other things?" Solly asked.

Mrs. Leer lifted a massive book from the trunk. It took both hands, for the book was as large as a dictionary. On the cover it said

INTERNATIONAL UNION OF EXTRAORDINARY CAREGIVERS

Official Rules, Regulations, and Procedures to Be Followed by All Members in Good Standing, Including Sanctions for All Infractions

"What's that mean?" Solly asked.

"I think it's the nanny rule book," I said.

"Quite so," said Mrs. Leer. "Of course, I know much of it by heart. But it makes soothing bedtime reading."

"Are sanctions the same as punishments?" I said.

"Yes, Eleanor. Ours is a most strict profession. And now, there is one more thing in that trunk."

Mrs. Leer put her hand in one last time and drew out a narrow leather pouch. She undid the drawstring and pulled something out.

"A flute!" Solly said.

"A tin whistle. After dear, dreary Mr. Leer passed on, I needed something to lift my spirits and keep my mind occupied. And I have always wanted to make music. But I could hardly lug a piano or a tuba around, could I? This was a present from a family I attended in Dublin, Ireland. Shall I give you a taste? Perhaps a round or two of the 'Swallowtail Jig'?"

Mrs. Leer put the end of the tin whistle to her lips, placed her fingers by the holes, and began to play. It was such a sweet, airy, lively sound that Solly started dancing right away. I thought myself too old to act ridiculous, so I just tapped my foot. And then nodded my head. And then, a moment later, I was dancing too.

6

LIGHTS, CAMERA, FLY!

I woke up every day and remembered that my parents weren't here. But I felt safe with Mrs. Leer. She was fun to be with, good at helping with homework, and a tasty cook too, even if she did make meals I'd never heard of from all the places around the world that she had visited. Solly liked Mrs. Leer just as much, but he was younger, after all, and naturally missed Mom and Dad even more. And then on Friday afternoon, I got called into the principal's office of Inkpotts Public School, where I found Solly sitting on a bench in his Googoo-man outfit, with a cold towel pressed to his bloody nose and a crack in his goggles.

"What happened?" I asked Solly.

"I gob indo a fight," he said, through the towel.

"A fight? Why?"

Solly wouldn't tell at first, but finally he gave in. Some boys had heard Solly trying to cheer himself up by singing his new Googoo-man theme song. They had started to sing it too, only they changed the words.

When you're in trouble, what do you do?
You call the guy who smells like poo.
He'll get you out, he'll stop the crime
Unless of course, it's his bedtime.

To be honest, I thought the words were kind of funny, but they were also mean, and when it came to Googoo-man, Solly didn't have much of a sense of humor. He was half their size, but he jumped those boys in the school-yard. I took him home and Mrs. Leer ran him a warm bubble bath.

"I do not approve of fighting as a way to solve problems," Mrs. Leer said, "but I can see that you do not need a lecture right now. You need some tender loving care. I'm going to make my specialty for dinner – chicken à la marsh-mallow – and afterwards, we'll play any game you like."

"Okay," sniffed Solly. "What country is chicken à la marshmallow from?"

"It is from the kingdom of the imagination. I just made it up now. It'll be interesting to see how it turns out."

How it turned out was very sticky. Afterwards, we watched TV and played a board game called Googoo-opoly. Solly had invented it. We watched Solly pick up cards that said things like, *You have just rescued a millionaire's baby. Collect a thousand dollars*, while Mrs. Leer and I picked up cards that said things like, *Googoo-man has caught you trying to rob the Hockey Hall of Fame. Go to jail and miss three turns.* Well, it was fun for him anyway.

On TV there was a report about *The Zoomers*. It showed a mail delivery truck arriving at the gates of Partankiss Productions and I.M. Partankiss taking the bags of mail. Then it showed him on the set of the show, opening an envelope and spilling the nickels inside on top of an enormous pile of coins. I.M. Partankiss said that half a million dollars had come in already, and it wouldn't be long before he could send the money to Verulia and get the show back on the air.

– *Remember, kids,* I.M. Partankiss said into the camera. *Zoomer toys can now be found in your neighborhood toy store. And the studio is still open for tours!*

After Solly was in bed asleep, Mrs. Leer made us some peppermint tea and we sat in the kitchen like two grown-ups. "Your poor brother," Mrs. Leer said. "He's taking your parents' absence very hard. Tomorrow is Saturday. We need to do something special, something to cheer him up. I thought maybe you'd have an idea of what he might like to do, Eleanor."

"I don't know," I said. But then a thought came to me. "Yes, I do know. Let's take him on a tour of Partankiss Productions. Solly loves that show, *The Zoomers*. He's asked my mom and dad to take us about a million times. He wants to see a real television studio."

"That is, indeed, an excellent idea. I knew I could count on you, Eleanor. And now, my dear, I think it is time for you to go to bed."

"Okay. Mrs. Leer?"

"Yes, Eleanor."

"I'm glad you're the one taking care of us."

"How very kind of you to say. And I am very, very glad to be here with you. Now give me a hug, my dear."

I did, and then I went to bed.

But I had trouble falling asleep. I wanted to fly, but Mom and Dad had forbidden us. Besides, the markings on my palm had faded away, except for the faint outline of two stars and a piece of the moon. Mom had given the amulet to Mrs. Leer, who had hung it on the picture frame of the dear, dreary Mr. Leer. Maybe I could reach in and just give it a squeeze. It wouldn't hurt to take a peek past her bedroom door and see. . . .

I crept down the hallway to my parents' bedroom. The door was open a crack. Listening, I could hear Mrs. Leer's delicate snore. She looked like a sound sleeper. I could feel that what I wanted to do was wrong, very wrong. But I pushed the feeling down and opened the door just enough to slip into the room.

It was so dark that I couldn't see a thing. My heart beat fast: *Go back, go back, go back*, it said, over and over. But I inched my way forward, feeling with my hands and feet. I came to the night table and felt the objects on top. A watch.

A comb. The picture frame. And then, yes, the necklace. I felt the shape of the amulet and pressed it into my hand.

The light blazed on. I dropped the amulet.

"Eleanor?"

Mrs. Leer had turned on the lamp. She sat up in bed with a hairnet on. "My goodness, child, what are you doing? It is very bad manners indeed to sneak into a person's room, or to go through their things. If you need me, you are always welcome to call for me, day or night. But to sneak about is an invasion of privacy."

"I'm sorry, Mrs. Leer."

"I'm disappointed, Eleanor. Now go back to bed."

I went out again, closing the door behind me. I knew that I shouldn't have done it. I felt just rotten; I didn't want her to think badly of me. Back in bed, I turned on my own lamp and looked into the palm of my hand. I'd just had time to give the amulet a quick squeeze, but the impression was there. Already faint, it would only last a day or so, but it was there.

When Mrs. Leer and I told Solly in the morning that we were going to take a tour of the Partankiss Productions' studio, he jumped for joy. I mean, he really did jump up and shout, "Oh joy, oh joy, oh joy." Then he ran into the bathroom and, when I finally went to fetch him, he was modeling his Googoo-man outfit in the bathroom mirror. "I want to look good," he said. "Maybe when the actors come back and the show starts up again, Kaspar Snit will put me in an episode. You know, a guest appearance by Googoo-man. I think he really liked me. I think he'd like to be my friend."

"If you say so."

Solly put on his goggles, which had a crack running across both lenses from his fight.

"Are you sure you want to wear those?" I said.

"Sure. They make it look like everything has been cut in half by a lightning bolt. It's really groovy, Melba."

"What did you call me?"

"Melba. I've decided that you need to be a new character."

"Huh?"

"I think you should be the newspaper reporter who writes all the stories about me and makes me famous. Your name's Melba Toast."

"You've got to be kidding."

"I'll tell you, Melba," Solly said, smiling into the mirror. "It wasn't easy stopping that train from smashing into the station. It took all my Googoo-strength. You want to feel my muscles?" He held up his skinny arm.

"No. You want to feel a kick in the pants? It's time to go."

Solly and I had to squeeze into the back of Mrs. Leer's tiny car. It was twenty years old, but in perfect condition.

"The dear, dreary Mr. Leer bought it for us," Mrs. Leer said. "He only liked to drive on Sundays. The rest of the time, he enjoyed being a passenger. So I acquired a taste for the road. All right, young Blandes. Strap yourselves in! We're ready for takeoff."

Solly and I looked at each other with wide eyes and buckled our seat belts. But instead of Mrs. Leer screeching away as we expected, she calmly turned on the signal light and then smoothly pulled onto the road.

"There are 147 regulations in the I.U.E.C. handbook devoted to driving," she told us. "And that includes never exceeding the speed limit. Ah, the pleasures of a late-spring outing – the wind in your face, the smell of daffodils in the air, the mad chirping of birds. According to the route that I mapped out last night, it should take us sixteen minutes to get there. Now, children, I am going to concentrate on my driving. So talk amongst yourselves."

"Okay, Mrs. Leer," Solly said. Then he turned to me. "So, Melba, you ask me what I think of Kaspar Snit turning into a good guy?"

"No, I didn't, actually."

"Well, I'll tell you. I'm disappointed. That's right, disappointed. I mean, sure there are lots of criminals out there – robbers, bullies, people who like to litter – but evil geniuses? They don't grow on trees you know."

"Thanks for the fascinating information. Should I write that down – evil geniuses don't grow on trees?"

"Right. Now, you ask whether I have any advice for all those young people out there who want to be superheroes. Well, I'll tell you. They should drink plenty of milk. Unless, of course, they're lactose-intolerant. Now you can take my picture for the front page."

"How about I just bonk you on the head and see if you come to your senses?"

"Melba," Solly said to me, "it sounds like you are having a bad day."

Five minutes later, Mrs. Leer pulled up in front of the gate of Partankiss Productions. Behind the gate, I could see the remains of Conlin's Amusement Park – the old roller coaster, the Ferris wheel. Beside the gate was a little booth, the sort a parking-lot attendant sits in, and the three of us got out of the car and went up to it. The man behind the glass was reading a newspaper called *The Racing Form*. He had a shaved head, a round nose, small eyes, and a little tuft of hair under his lower lip. Right away I recognized him as the actor who played the villain on *The Zoomers*.

The man put down his newspaper and slid open the glass window.

"Hey, you're Karl Snoop," Solly said.

"I'm the actor who plays Karl Snoop," the man said. "My name is Marvin Slouch. Don't you read the credits? I've also played Hamlet. I've played Julius Caesar. But nobody ever recognizes me from them."

"We're sure you were very good," Mrs. Leer said. "May we please have three tickets for the studio tour?"

"Now you're talking. Three adult tickets at twenty bucks each."

"Three adults? But I've got two children here."

"Are they more than three days old?"

"Of course they are."

"Then they're adults. That'll be eighty-four dollars."

"But three times twenty dollars is sixty, not eighty-four."

"We've added a fee for the makeup artist retirement fund. Unless you think makeup artists don't deserve to retire?"

"Of course they do. Let me look in my wallet."

"Plus there's a two-dollar handling fee."

"My word."

"And a three-dollar arts tax."

"But that's eighty-nine dollars!"

"Oh, I almost forgot. There's a one-dollar charge for explaining the charges."

"Well, I'm sorry, but I've got only fifteen dollars in my wallet."

"I'll take it." He snatched the money out of Mrs. Leer's hand. "Go right in. Straight to Misery Mountain and knock loud on the door. Have fun."

The man in the booth turned a crank and the gate opened with an awful screech. "Just follow the carpet," he shouted, as we went through.

The carpet was gold and stretched from the other side of the gate all the way to Misery Mountain. We walked along it, past remains of the amusement park strewn on either side with a pair of big clown shoes, milk bottles and wooden rings from midway games, an empty candy-floss cart. The artificial mountain loomed larger and Solly came up beside me and took my hand. Like me, he was starting to feel anxious. After all, this was Kaspar Snit territory and, although he had reformed, the thought of him still made me shiver.

From far away the mountain looked real, and on television too, but up close it was only plaster and chicken wire and paint. There was a plain door in the side with a doorbell on it.

"Go ahead and ring the bell," Solly said to me.

"No, you ring it."

"No, you."

"Goodness sakes, children. I shall ring it," Mrs. Leer said. She pushed the button. Immediately the door swung open to show a man in a flashy blue suit and matching blue cowboy hat. "Welcome to Partankiss Productions! Come in and see how a real television show is made!"

It took me a moment to realize that the man was the very same person who had sold us the tickets. Marvin Slouch. Now he led us down a bright corridor to show us the makeup and dressing rooms. The dressing rooms had big mirrors surrounded by lightbulbs. On a rack I could see all the superhero outfits of the Zoomers. Solly immediately went over to feel the cape on Zoomer-boy's outfit.

"Nice material," he said admiringly.

"Come away from there now," said our guide. "There's no time to dawdle. It's on to the sets. First you'll see the exterior of the Zoomer house and then all the rooms."

We followed him into a very large space that was underneath the peak of the mountain. I could see the mountain's metal structure rise above us and, at the peak, a blue circle of light that must have been a hole, or a skylight, at the very top. When I looked down again, I was amazed to see the Zoomers' house – at least the front of it, for it was just a flat front with nothing behind. But with the bushes, mailbox, and even a full-size tree with a swing, it all looked amazingly real. I went up close and saw that the tree was made of papier-mâché. The bricks on the house were painted Styrofoam. Everything looked real, and everything was fake.

"Quite fascinating, isn't it, children?" Mrs. Leer said. "And I believe it all looks even more real on television. But it's no more real than a dream."

"Right you are. So tell me, ma'am, which is your favorite character on *The Zoomers*?"

"I'm afraid I've never seen it. I don't watch television. There are so many other interesting things to do with one's time."

"Well, there's an attitude we wouldn't like to see get spread around. Now, don't stop! Come along. Just over here are all the interior rooms. The living room, dining room, kitchen, and even the bedrooms. Karl Snoop's laboratory, too."

"Wow," Solly said.

Wow was right. The rooms looked so real, except they had no ceilings or front walls, and they were right beside each other in a row. In front of them was a kind of miniature train track for the camera, which was mounted on wheels and could slide back and forth. Solly went onto the set of the kids' room and I could see him frown when he realized that everything in the Zoomer kids' room – the stereo, the computer – was just a shell. Even the boxes of toys were empty.

"It's all make-believe," Solly said.

"Of course it is!" said Marvin Slouch. "Like the lady said, it's no more real than a dream. But look over here. We have the highlight of the tour. This is how we make the Zoomers fly."

Actually, there were two ways to make it look as if the Zoomers were flying. To show them taking off or landing, the actors wore special harnesses under their costumes, attached to thin metal wires. The wires were attached to a crane that could lift the actors up or lower them down. With proper lighting, the wires couldn't be seen. The other way was used to show them flying through the sky. The actors had to lie on special platforms. While a moving background showed distant mountains, or the city down below, a large fan would blow their hair and capes.

"Young man," said Marvin Slouch to Solly, "why don't you lie down on one of those platforms and I'll point the camera at you. Then you can see yourself in the television monitor."

"Cool," Solly said. He practically jumped onto the platform. The man got behind the large camera and a green light came on. A moment later, we all saw Solly on the television screen, looking as if he were flying. Solly stroked his arms through the air and then turned over.

"Lights, camera, fly! Look, I'm doing the backstroke!"

"Very funny. All right, you can get down from there."

"Anyway, it doesn't feel like real flying. I want to look at the Zoomers' house again."

"That is going in the wrong direction."

But Solly didn't care. He ran back to the Zoomers' house and pushed on the swing that hung from the fake tree. "This is weird," he said. "Look, Eleanor, there's a kind of doorway in the back of the tree. See the hinges?"

"Don't mess about with that, young man," Marvin Slouch said. He walked over to Solly and pulled him away from the tree. "There are electrical wires in there. You might get a shock. You must never, ever open that door."

"Okay."

"I mean never. I mean, there's nothing in there except what I've told you. It's not as if I'm hiding something."

"Ah, sure."

"Now, if you'll just come this way, you'll enter the Partankiss Productions' souvenir shop. We have the full line of Zoomer toys as well as mugs, T-shirts, towels, key chains, caps, car deodorizers, and photographs of the stars, all at very reasonable prices."

Solly said, "You don't by any chance have a whoopie cushion with a picture of I.M. Partankiss on it?"

"I'm afraid not."

"And where is I.M. Partankiss anyway? Don't we get to meet the creator of *The Zoomers*?"

"Now, Solly," said Mrs. Leer. "I'm sure Mr. Partankiss is very busy."

"Yes, he is. Very busy."

We walked through the shop, but didn't buy anything and, a moment later, we were at the door again. Just as Marvin Slouch was letting us out, a little postal service van pulled up. A mailman hopped out of the cab and, from the back of the truck, pulled out five heavy bags of letters. I could hear all the coins jingling as he put them by the door.

"I know what I.M. Partankiss is doing, Mr. Slouch," Solly said. "He's counting all the money."

"That's right!" said Marvin Slouch. "Counting so that we can send it to Verulia. And when we get to a million dollars, you'll be able to watch your favorite TV show again. Just call me Slouch. I don't suppose you'd like to contribute?"

"It's a worthy cause, but I don't have any money left," said Mrs. Leer.

"We sent money," Solly said. "But I also brought all the money in my piggy bank."

"Excellent," said Slouch, rubbing his hands together. "How much is that, exactly?"

Solly fished the money out of his pajama pocket. "Forty-three cents. One of the pennies is bent, but I think it's still good."

Slouch frowned. "Well, hand it over."

Solly poured the money into Slouch's hand.

"It's all sticky," Slouch said.

"Sorry. Melted Popsicle."

"And I have ten dollars," I said quietly. I, too, had

brought my money. I wanted to help all those people in Verulia as much as Solly did.

"Ah, that's a pretty amount." Slouch grinned, taking the bill from me. Then he carefully folded it into a small square, put it in his mouth, and chewed. When he opened his mouth, the bill was gone.

"A lovely impulse from the both of you," Mrs. Leer said. "To give, in order to help others. Mr. Slouch, thank you for the tour. It was most educational. Now, children, back into the Leermobile."

I guess I was relieved not to see Kaspar Snit in his guise as I.M. Partankiss, but I think that I was a little disappointed too. That night, lying in bed, I imagined coming upon him in the studio, Kaspar Snit in his new beret and diamond-studded cape, maybe writing a script for the next show.

> *– Why, Eleanor Blande. I can't believe it! Please sit down. Can I get you something? A cola? Hot chocolate? Fancy French mineral water? I'm so glad you're here. Because I want to thank you, Eleanor. I want to thank you for helping me to see the error of my ways. You know what? I'm glad that you and your family foiled my evil plans. I'm glad that I had to spend time in that awful jail. It's because of you that I've found my true calling. Now I'm a writer and director and producer. I express myself creatively rather than through evil. People like my show. They even like me! And I owe all of it to you, Eleanor. . . .*

"Eleanor?"

It was Solly in my doorway. *Did he have to ruin a good dream?* "What is it?" I asked.

He came over to my bed. "I keep thinking."

"About what?"

"About that door in the tree. Something was fishy about it. And why would he say there was nothing hidden behind it unless there actually *was* something hidden behind it? I'm going to go back."

"I really doubt that Mrs. Leer will take us back for another tour."

"No, not that way. I'm going to fly back. Tonight."

"Fly! But we're not supposed to. Besides, you don't have any markings left on your palm."

"I do so. Look." He held out his palm and I could see the markings faintly. "I've just got enough to fly tonight. By tomorrow morning, it'll be too late."

"It's not safe. I'm your older sister and I say forget it."

Solly grinned at me. "I'll let you know what I find. See you!"

He sprinted out of my room. "Solly!" I whispered loudly, for I didn't want to wake up Mrs. Leer. But he didn't answer. I pushed off my covers, got out of bed, and walked down the hall to the living room.

The window was open. Solly was gone.

7

MISERY MOUNTAIN

I ran to the window and looked out. There he was, already over the trees. A moment later, he was out of sight. I suddenly remembered my mother and father's words before leaving. *Keep an eye on Solly. You know what mischief he can get into.* They had asked me to do only one thing and I had blown it already. I just couldn't let him fly all the way to Partankiss Productions by himself. But how could I stop him? Waking Mrs. Leer wouldn't do any good and, besides, I'd have to tell her that we could fly. I would just have to go after him myself. It was a good thing that I had grabbed the amulet. Now I went to the window, closed my eyes, put my hands in position, and . . . *whoosh.* I was in the air, hovering over the house.

"Step on the gas," I told myself, and a moment later I was moving at top speed through the night sky. After a few moments, I could make out a dot in the sky ahead of me that must have been Solly. But he was going at least as fast as me and I wasn't catching up. Past the Rooster's Fried Chicken, the hockey arena, the water tower. I started to feel tired, but I couldn't let up or I would lose Solly. Another ten minutes and the old amusement park came into view, with Misery Mountain rising in the middle.

By the time I got there, Solly had already descended. I could see him on the ground, looking around and then stepping towards the front door. Convincing himself that he really was Googoo-man made him more brave than it was safe for him to be. He was trying to figure out his next move. I decided to descend and force him to come home. But just as I was coming down, the door into the mountain flung open and two arms reached out. They grabbed Solly and yanked him inside before the door slammed shut again.

Solly grabbed! I felt an awful panic, but I didn't know what to do. If I went to the door, I might get grabbed too. I tried to think of some other way in. Hadn't I seen something when I was inside? Yes, a round circle of light, an open space at the very peak of the mountain. Maybe I could look down through it.

I flew upwards again, following the mountain's rise, all the way to the top. A pigeon was circling the hole and I had to shoo it away. Luckily the builders had put some metal footholds around the peak, so that as I landed, I had a way to hang on. Yes, there was a hole at the very top, about the size of, well, a toilet seat. Holding on to the peak and looking in, I could see straight down into the sets for *The Zoomers*. I saw Solly walk into view, with Marvin Slouch just behind him, poking Solly with his finger to make him hurry up. Then, from the other direction, someone else was coming.

Kaspar Snit.

"Well, well, what an unexpected treat," Kaspar Snit said. "We weren't expecting any visitors at this time of night, were we, Slouch? But an old friend is always welcome. I'm only sorry you didn't bring your charming sister along with you."

"Yeah, well, she had to catch up on her comic-book reading," Solly said, trying to sound brave. "So what do I call you, anyway? I.M. Partankiss, or your real name – Kaspar Snit? It doesn't matter to me. I can even call you Snitty."

"Don't call me Snitty!" Kaspar Snit bellowed. "They called me that in school. 'What's the matter, Snitty-Snotty, miss your mother?' I hated it."

"Okay, okay, I get the picture."

I could see Kaspar Snit calming himself down. He stroked his mustache. "Excuse me. It's still rather a soft spot. Won't you sit down here in the Zoomer living room? The sofa is quite comfortable. I don't believe we need you, Slouch. Find something useful to do."

Slouch, as Kaspar Snit called him, nodded and backed away. Solly went over to the sofa and sat. He sank into the pillows, making him look even smaller. "So," he said, "you're a TV big shot now."

"Some people think so. I just try to create quality programming."

"It's a pretty good show. I mean, sometimes the stories aren't very believable. And the kids are definitely too goody-goody. And every episode is exactly like all the others. But, otherwise, it's great. Would you mind if I make a suggestion?"

"Everyone's a critic. Well, go ahead."

"I think you should give Zoomer-boy a bigger part in the stories. I mean, he's the most interesting, and the funniest too. I bet it would boost your ratings."

"Do you now. Well, I'll give it my most serious consideration."

"You don't have a cookie or something around here, do you? A piece of chocolate cake, maybe?"

"This is not a snack bar. Now, if you don't mind my asking, exactly what are you doing here?"

"Good question," Solly said, leaning back and crossing his legs. "You see, I think it's really great that you've gotten out of the bad-guy business. But as Googoo-man, I have to be pretty careful. You know, follow up on things. I remember how much you liked doing evil, how fun and exciting it was to you. And it seems to me that you were the sort of evil genius – don't take this personally – who might like to get revenge for being defeated." Solly stood up and wandered across the living room. "On our tour today, I noticed this little door in the fake tree over here. I asked myself, 'Why would a tree have a door in it?' Sure, houses have doors. Schools, libraries. But trees? Not too often. So that's when I decided to come back and . . . run for it!"

I couldn't believe what I was seeing. Solly sprinted across the set, leapt over a chair, and ran to the tree. I thought that Kaspar Snit would run after him, but he didn't; he just watched as Solly grabbed the doorknob and yanked on it. I wished that I could see Kaspar Snit's expression, but I was too high up. Solly yanked and yanked, but the door wouldn't budge. Finally he stopped trying and turned back to Kaspar Snit. Solly looked at him and then lowered his eyes.

"You tricked me, didn't you?" he said.

Kaspar Snit chuckled.

"You wanted me to come back. And you," he pointed to Slouch, "you wanted me to see that you were hiding something."

"Clever, aren't I?" Kaspar Snit said. "Slouch, take away those pathetic Googoo-weapons. They might seem harmless, but I know better this time."

I watched Slouch pull the weapons from Solly's belt – his electromagnetic scrambler and his force-field generator. Just as he turned around, I thought I saw G.W.'s nose poke out from the pocket in Solly's cape. Slouch must have seen something too, because he turned back. But then he shook his head and took away the weapons.

"You're so very right about one thing, peewee," Kaspar Snit said to Solly. "I do like evil. It *is* exciting. It *is* glamorous. And," his voice deepened, "I do want vengeance."

The sound of his voice – the mean, cruel voice that I remembered – sent a chill through me. Something fluttered in my face, making me let go to protect myself. It was the pigeon. I had leaned backwards too far and now I felt myself sliding down the side of the mountain.

8

A CAD, A SCALLYWAG, AND A NOGOODNIK

I couldn't find anything to hold on to and stop my fall. I bumped, slid, bounced, and somersaulted all the way back down to the ground. Lying on my face, I felt bruised and sore, but I had no time to moan or check myself over. I had to get home and tell Mrs. Leer. I pulled myself up, got in position, closed my eyes, and rose into the air.

I never felt so desperate while flying, and desperation, as I found out, is not a good mental state to be in when airborne. Instead of flying in a smooth line forward, my body kept dipping and rising again, like an aeroplane with a stuttering engine. I felt so glad to see our house down below that I almost cried.

A moment later, I felt the living-room carpet under my grateful feet. I was so tired that my legs folded under me and I landed in a heap. Mrs. Leer must have heard me, because a moment later she came into the living room and helped me up.

"My dear Eleanor, what are you doing on the floor? Are you feeling all right?"

"Mrs. Leer, we've got to save Solly."

"Wake Solly? But it's almost midnight. You need to go to bed, Eleanor."

"Not wake him, *save* him. He went back to the mountain – to Partankiss Productions. And now Kaspar Snit's got him."

"Who's got Solly?"

"Kaspar Snit."

"Isn't he that awful man who stole the fountains of Rome? I read about it in the newspapers. But what would he want with Solly? And what is he doing in a television studio?"

"We just have to get in the car. I'll explain along the way."

"Dear Eleanor," Mrs. Leer said, "why don't we check Solly's room?"

When Mrs. Leer found Solly's bed empty, she grew as worried as I was. "We'll go to the police," she said, and sent me to get dressed quickly. She did the same and then, as we drove in her little car, I told her how we'd discovered that Kaspar Snit had stolen the fountains; how we ended up captives in his fortress in Verulia; and how we had defeated him with the help of Googoo-man's neutronic knocker. It wasn't easy leaving out the part about being able to fly, but Mrs. Leer was too anxious to notice any gaps in the story. And she was concentrating hard on driving. She was even going five miles over the speed limit!

"According to I.U.E.C. regulation 173-B," she told me, "'when a child under your charge is in danger, moderate speeding is permitted while driving, except when it may cause a hazard to others.'" Fortunately the streets were empty at midnight.

"Eleanor," Mrs. Leer said, "I am shocked and appalled by the behavior of this dastardly Carlton Snoot."

"It's Kaspar Snit."

"Whatever. Here we are. I'll pull right up and we'll just go in and explain ourselves."

Mrs. Leer parked the car in front of the police station and out we got. It was an old redbrick building, with the words TO SERVE AND PROTECT carved in stone over the door. Well, if anyone needed protecting right now, it was Solly.

Inside, the floor was worn linoleum and the walls needed painting. There were real WANTED posters on the walls, with frowning men and women glaring at us as we walked by. Mrs. Leer took my arm and hurried us up the hall to the front desk, where a police officer was eating a hero sandwich and flipping through the sports section of the newspaper.

"Excuse me, officer," Mrs. Leer said. "We have an emergency situation. Here. Kasbard Snoot –"

"Kaspar Snit," I said.

"Yes, yes, Kaspar Snit has kidnapped Solly. He's holding him captive in Misery Mountain."

Calmly the police officer closed the newspaper. He wiped a streak of mustard off his face. "Let me get this straight," he said. "Somebody is holding someone in Mount something or other."

"It's I.M. Partankiss," I blurted out, "who makes the television show *The Zoomers.* Except that he isn't really I.M. Partankiss. He's the man who stole all the fountains of Rome. Kaspar Snit."

"Must have happened when I was off duty," the police officer said, with a smile.

"He's got my brother, Solly."

"Okay," the officer said. "So what you're telling me is, your brother has run away from home. Did he have an argument with your parents? Didn't get the toy he wanted, maybe? So we need to file a missing person's report and then alert all the squad cars –"

"No, no!" I insisted. "They won't find him. Mrs. Leer already said, he's in Misery Mountain."

"I don't know if you've noticed, young lady, but we don't have any mountains around here."

"It's not a real mountain. It's fake."

"Oh, well, that explains it. Now everything is crystal clear," the police officer said, taking another bite of sandwich. "Is this some kind of joke? Did Detective Skeet put you up to this? That kidder, always trying to get me. Or, is this your own idea? You know, it's a serious offense to put in a false report."

"Officer, thank you for your help," Mrs. Leer said, pulling on my arm. "Come along, Eleanor. We've wasted enough of the officer's time."

"But we've got to do something. . . ."

Mrs. Leer pulled me down the hall and outside again. "It's no good," she said. "He doesn't believe us. And who can blame him? Come on, Eleanor, get back in the car."

She opened the door for me and I got in. Then she went around to the other side, got in, started the car, and began driving again. "There's only one thing to do," she said. "We'll have to go to Partankiss Productions ourselves."

"But what will we do then?"

"We'll simply insist that he hand Solly over, or face the consequences. He may have had to face the Italian police before; he may even have had to face television network executives. But he has not faced a card-carrying member of the International Union of Extraordinary Caregivers. Let him just try to refuse. Hang on, Eleanor, I'm making a hard right!"

Mrs. Leer swung the car around and took off. It took us twenty more minutes to pull up in front of the gate of Partankiss Productions. Mrs. Leer got out of the car and I followed, as she strode with determination up to the gate. "Locked," she said. "Well, I don't expect there's any use in shouting. You're small enough to squeeze under, Eleanor, but there's twice too much of me. I'll have to go over the top. Give me a boost, will you, dear?"

"But, Mrs. Leer . . ."

"Come on, there isn't a moment to lose."

I cupped my hands and Mrs. Leer put her big foot on them. "Heave-ho!" she called, and I pushed up while she pulled on the top of the gate. To my surprise, she lifted right out of my hands and over the gate, landing on the other side. "My nanny-training stands me in good stead," she said, wiping the dust from her hands. "Now come on, Eleanor, don't dillydally. We've got your brother to save."

I crawled underneath and met Mrs. Leer on the other side. Marching again, we followed the gold carpet right up to the door set into the side of Misery Mountain. "Now, Eleanor," she said. "I think it best if I confront this fellow. You hide behind that abandoned hot-dog cart. This will be a good lesson for you in how to deal with difficult people. You need to speak with authority and confidence."

"But, Mrs. Leer, you don't know Kaspar Snit. He's not like –"

"Tut-tut, my dear. I've had more experience in my lifetime than you can possibly imagine. Go on now, hide yourself."

I did what Mrs. Leer asked, but I didn't feel good about it. She checked that I was behind the cart before rapping hard on the door and calling out in a loud voice, "Open up, do you hear me? This instant. As a member in good standing of the International Union of Extraordinary

Caregivers, I demand that you return my charge. Open up, I say! Or I shall resort . . ."

Mrs. Leer didn't finish her sentence because the door opened. There stood Slouch, who I realized by now must be Kaspar Snit's assistant in his evil plans.

"It's rather late. May I help you?" he said innocently.

"I would like to speak to Captain Snipe."

"Who?"

"I mean Karlsbad Slope."

"Perhaps you mean Kaspar Snit."

"That's what I said."

"I'm afraid that he is writing poetry and can't be disturbed."

"If you hand over Solly, I will be satisfied."

"What is a Solly?"

"The boy."

"There are no boys here. No boys, no girls, no rabbits, and no fish, either."

"I see you for what you are, sir," Mrs. Leer said haughtily. "You are a miscreant and a recidivist."

"Huh?"

"An offender of the law, many times over."

"Now that isn't a nice thing to say."

"You leave me no choice but to use even harsher words and perhaps a little force." Mrs. Leer reached forward and grabbed Slouch by the nose.

"Ouch! Wet go ub me."

"Give me back Solly."

"Okee, okee, den come intide."

"That's better," said Mrs. Leer, and she let go of his nose. When she stepped inside, immediately the door slammed behind her. Then came the sound of Kaspar Snit's awful laugh, like black smoke twirling upwards.

Mrs. Leer was trapped inside too! She had been fooled just as much as Solly had. *What was I supposed to do?* I came out from behind the hot-dog cart, closed my eyes, and hoped that the outline of my hand hadn't faded. A moment later, I was rising up the side of the mountain. Fortunately, there wasn't anyone in the grounds to see me. Approaching the top, I saw that pesky pigeon, this time perched on the edge of the hole. "Go away!" I hissed. I came down on the footholds, grabbing the edge of the hole. As soon as I landed, I could hear Mrs. Leer's outraged voice.

"You, Kandy Sweet, are a cad. Yes, a cad, and a scallywag to boot. And also, if I might add, a nogoodnik."

Looking down, I could see Mrs. Leer standing with one arm around Solly. Kaspar Snit was standing by the artificial tree and Slouch was hovering behind him.

"I would appreciate it if you got my name right, madam. It is not Sweet, or Slope, or Snipe, or anything else besides Snit. Kaspar Snit. You should learn it, madam, just as the whole world will soon remember it. And exactly who are you to call people names?" he sneered. "I must say, I am most distressed by my old friends Manfred and Daisy. I have always taken them to be exemplary parents, and here I discover that they have left their precious children in the care of a nanny who is clearly incompetent."

"She is not incompetent!" Solly said. "Whatever that means."

"Thank you, dear boy," Mrs. Leer said, "but I am sorry to say that, in this instance, Mr. . . . uh . . . Snit is correct. You were my responsibility. There is no excuse for my losing you. Or my ending up here myself. As for you, Mr. Snit, you ought to be ashamed of yourself. I can just imagine the sort of naughty know-it-all boy you once were. Pulling heads off grasshoppers. Putting salt in the grown-ups' tea and chewing gum on your teacher's seat. Thinking that you were better than everyone else. And lonely."

Kaspar Snit took a step back. "How do you know all that?"

"Oh, I've seen all types of children. You are nothing new to me, Mr. Snit. Unfortunately, there was no grown-up able to take you in hand when you needed it. Someone to be both firm and loving. And so the nasty boy, left unchecked, grows into the nasty man. It is a real tragedy."

"A tragedy?" grumbled Kaspar Snit. "Why do you say that?"

"Because of the promise that you must have had. You were a clever boy, weren't you? Perfect marks on your tests without even studying. Putting toys and kits together without the instructions. Yes, it's a tragedy to see your talents wasted."

"Ah, but that is where you are wrong, Mrs. Leer. They're not wasted at all. Now, why don't we all sit down and have something to eat?"

"It's not morning yet," said Mrs. Leer.

"Surely a snack won't hurt. I think the Zoomers' dining-room table will serve us quite nicely."

"I bet I can get there first," Solly said.

"I really don't think so," said Kaspar Snit. "But I have no intention of racing a child in a ridiculous costume."

"Scared of losing?"

"Oh, please, that sort of thing only works in the playground."

"Okay, be last then. One . . . two . . . *three!*"

Solly raced off towards the dining-room set. And so did Kaspar Snit, his cape flying behind him. "I'm gaining on you!" Kaspar Snit cried, and they both slid towards the chairs.

"Got here first," Solly said.

"You did not."

"Did so."

"Did not."

"Crybaby spoilsport."

"You're the crybaby –"

"Really!" said Mrs. Leer, as she walked up behind them. "Mr. Snit, I would expect someone as evil as you to at least act your age. You are hardly an example for the boy."

Kaspar Snit stood straight and fixed his cape. "Madam, you are right. That boy brings out the worst in me. Slouch, serve the meal."

"Yes, boss."

Kaspar Snit pulled out a chair for Mrs. Leer and then sat down himself. Solly sat down too, and he and Kaspar

Snit glared at each other. Then Kaspar Snit turned to Mrs. Leer.

"We have a kitchen to make meals in when we are rehearsing and taping a new show. Ah, here is Slouch. What have you made for us?"

Slouch was carrying a big steaming pot. "You'll love it," he said. "A little recipe of my own invention. Oatmeal with asparagus and a mushroom-raisin sauce. Smells yummy, doesn't it?"

Kaspar Snit put on a strained smile. "It's difficult to find good help."

Slouch served the oatmeal – it looked gooey, even from up here – and they picked up their spoons. I watched Solly take a taste. "Hey, it's not bad," he said. "Next time, throw in some chocolate chips. I've got an idea. It's so thick, we can stick candles into it and sing 'Happy Birthday.' "

"I don't celebrate birthdays," Kaspar Snit said.

"That's okay, it's nobody's birthday anyway." Solly pretended to blow out a candle and then started to sing.

Happy birthday to you,
We're eating gross stew.
Kaspar Snit thinks he's got us,
But he'll be beaten by Goo!

"That's it, you little Googoo-twerp!" Kaspar Snit snarled. "I've had enough of you."

Kaspar Snit leaned over the table and grabbed Solly's collar, lifting him half out of his chair.

Solly! I leaned forward, into the hole, as if I might be able to reach down and rescue him. But I couldn't.

Mrs. Leer stood up. "Unhand that boy!"

"You can't hurt me!" Solly said, although I heard how scared he was. "Right at this very minute, my sister, Eleanor, is bringing help. She knows all about us being here. She's smart. She's practical. She's bringing the police right now, or the army maybe, and when they get here, just see what happens. . . ."

Oh, Solly, if only you were right. In fact, that's what I ought to have done – returned to the police. I moved my foot to back away, but then something came right up in front of me and began flapping in my face. It was that darn pigeon again. I batted at it with my hands and the pigeon darted down into the hole. Suddenly I tipped forward. I tried to grab the edge, but my hands slipped off and I plunged through the hole after the pigeon. A second later, I was tumbling down through the air.

9

ELEANOR DROPS IN

I didn't mean to, but as I fell I started to scream. It was a long way and I would have broken a lot of bones, or worse, if I hadn't instinctively put my hands to my side and closed my eyes. The markings on my hand were so faded that I could just manage to lower myself gently down. When I opened my eyes again, I was standing beside a malevolent-looking Kaspar Snit.

"Eleanor Blande!"

"I hope I'm not interrupting," I said sheepishly.

"Eleanor!" Solly cried. I had never seen him look more happy to see me. Mrs. Leer, on the other hand, looked absolutely stunned. Speechless, in fact. But then, she'd never seen me fly before. She'd never seen *anybody* fly.

"Did you bring the police?" Solly asked. "Are we going to hear sirens any minute?"

"I, uh, well, no, I didn't."

"How about the army?"

"No."

"Not even a bunch of Boy Scouts with pointed sticks?"

"I'm sorry."

"That's all right, dear," Mrs. Leer said, coming over to put her arm around me. "You can't be expected to think of everything. That was supposed to be my job."

"Well," Solly said, "at least you're in time for dessert."

Kaspar Snit gave me his most sinister smile. "I'm very glad you've joined us, Eleanor. In fact, I was counting on your dropping in. That was a very impressive landing you made. You see, while I know that Solly, too, can fly, he's a little immature, shall we say, and not likely to be a good teacher. But you will be an excellent one."

"Teacher?" I said.

"Instructor, coach – call it whatever you want. The point is, my dear Eleanor, that I need you to show me just one thing. How to fly."

"To fly?"

"Your repetitions are becoming tedious. Yes, Eleanor, you are going to teach me to fly. Indeed, that is why you are here. Do you think that being merely a television director – a wildly successful one, I might add – could possibly satisfy my need for power, for infamy? Just think of the evil that I could do if only I had your little talent for being airborne. Why, it makes me shiver with pleasure just to contemplate it. Swooping down on people in the night, causing fear and chaos. And now," Kaspar Snit said, standing up, "this meal is over. Slouch, settle our guests in. They can occupy *The Zoomers*' set. After all, the beds are real. If you'll excuse me, I have a great deal of money to count."

Not even Solly could think of a wisecrack. We watched Kaspar Snit as he knocked over the chair and walked away, his cape billowing behind him.

Slouch took us to the bedrooms of *The Zoomers*' set. "Don't lean on the walls," he said. "They'll fall over. And don't try to turn on the lamps because they don't really work. And the books don't have any words in them. Otherwise, make yourselves at home."

Solly cheered up a little when he realized that he was going to sleep in the same bunk bed as Zoomer-boy, and I let him choose the top. Mrs. Leer settled him in. Slouch was turning away when I said, "Can I ask you a question?"

He turned back. "Is it a hard question, like three hundred and twenty-seven divided by one hundred and eighty-four? Because I hate hard questions."

"No, it's not like that. Why do you work for Kaspar Snit?"

Slouch looked at me and then took a toothpick out of his pocket and slipped it between his teeth. He leaned an elbow casually against a wall, but when it started to shake, he stood up again. "Listen, kid," he said. "Let me tell you *Slouch's Guide to Getting Along in this World*."

"You have a guide?"

"That's right. Number one, you got to know the truth about life, which is this: Life is a contest."

"A contest?"

"A contest. And you're either gonna be a winner, or you're gonna be a loser. Me, I prefer to be a winner. And how do you win? Well, you can be born rich, which isn't me. You can be smarter than everyone else, which also isn't me. You can have some amazing talent that everyone wants to pay to see. But you know what?"

"That isn't you either?"

"Bingo. So if you don't have any of those things, there's only one option. You find somebody who does. I found Kaspar Snit. I made myself useful to him. If there is anyone who is talented at being evil, it's him. He's got the brains, he's got the ambition, and instead of a human heart inside him, he's got a moldy onion. Maybe he was down for a while, but Kaspar Snit's going to be a winner. And I'm going to be a winner with him."

"He doesn't treat you very well."

"Why would he? He's not a nice person. It makes him feel good to be mean to me. That's part of my job."

"Then it's a pretty crummy job."

"You know who I was before I joined Kaspar Snit? I was Marvin Slouchovsky, third-rate at everything. Even after I became an actor, things didn't get better. You know what the highlight of my career was before *The Zoomers*? I was the third pickle from the right in the Riznik Dill Pickle commercial. I was getting nowhere fast. On my way to Loserville, do not pass go, do not collect two hundred dollars. And now? I'm Slouch. I've got one name, like a rock star. I'm somebody, a winner."

"I think you're wrong," I said. "I don't think that there have to be just winners and losers in life."

Slouch took the toothpick from his lips and pointed it at me. "Kid," he said, turning to go, "you've got a lot to learn."

Mrs. Leer was to sleep in the room next to ours, the one that was supposed to belong to the Zoomer parents. There were still a few hours before morning, so she got Solly tucked in, and leaned down to the bottom bunk to fix my blanket. "So tell me, can you actually fly, or just float to the ground?"

"Oh, I can fly," I said. "But right now all my power's used up. It's kind of a long story."

"Well, you can tell me later. Right now it's time for rest. I'll sleep with my ears open," she said. "If you need anything, just call."

"Mrs. Leer," Solly said. "Do you have your tin whistle with you?"

"Why, yes, my dear, I put it in my long vest pocket. I like to keep it with me, you see."

"Would you play something soft while you're in bed? It might help me to go to sleep."

"All right," she said, tucking his blanket around him. Then she went into her own room and, a couple of minutes later, a slow mournful tune drifted in. I thought that Kaspar Snit might come and make her stop, but he didn't appear.

Solly was exhausted and he fell asleep right away; I could hear him whistle through the gap in his teeth as he breathed. And I could hear something else – a soft cooing sound. It was the pigeon, which had come in through the hole. After a while, Mrs. Leer stopped playing. But I lay on the lower bunk, thinking about my mom and dad. I wondered what they were doing right now. In Italy, it was already morning. Maybe they were sitting at some café, eating Italian ice cream with long spoons. Maybe they were standing in a square, watching a street performer riding a unicycle while juggling flaming torches and spinning a plate on his head. Whatever they were doing, it was sure more fun than this. I thought, *You see what happens when you leave your children behind? They get captured by an evil genius! They have to eat oatmeal with mushrooms! And sleep in fake rooms!*

This wasn't getting me anywhere. Instead, I started to think about Kaspar Snit's demand that we teach him how to fly. I didn't see how we could refuse him, but on the other hand, we had to keep the power of flying out of his grasp. The question was, how?

At some point everything faded to a blur and I fell asleep in Zoomer-girl's bed. It didn't feel like more than a few minutes before I was woken by Slouch, banging a metal spoon against a pot and calling, "Wakey, wakey! Time to get up! Kaspar Snit has plans for you."

I got up just as Mrs. Leer came in, but Solly was still fast asleep. Gently I shook his shoulder. "Wake up, Solly."

"Yes, I will have some more Turkish delight," he mumbled.

"Solly, you're dreaming," I said. "Get up."

Solly opened his eyes. "What? You're not the White Witch? You're not making me king?"

Solly got out of bed and Slouch showed us to the bathroom on the set, so that we could wash up. Then he took us to Kaspar Snit, who was waiting by the artificial tree. He wore his black cape with diamonds, and black trousers, and black boots, and his mustache was waxed and perfectly curled.

"Ah, our guests are up. I trust you slept well?"

"I slept great," Solly said. "Can I take that bed home with me?"

"No."

"Okay, then when's breakfast? I'm starved."

"Hunger seems to be your regular state. However, a meal is coming up. But first, there's something I'd like you to see."

Kaspar Snit took a step closer to the artificial tree and opened the door in its trunk. "I knew it opened!" said Solly.

"You think you're clever?" Kaspar Snit said. "It's a door, of course it opens. But what is down below? That is the question. I shall lead the way. Mrs. Leer, if you will follow, and then Eleanor and Solly. Slouch will be right behind you."

"So no funny business," Slouch said.

"Slouch, try not to speak like you're in a very bad movie," Kaspar Snit said. "On our way, then."

It wasn't dark inside the trunk as I'd expected because there was a lamp glowing on the inside wall. There was just enough room for a winding metal staircase, which we took down under the ground. At the bottom was another door. Kaspar Snit said, "Let me introduce you to the first family of flight." He opened the door to what looked like a regular basement rec room, with wood paneling on the walls, old sofas, a black-and-white television, a stereo, even a Ping-Pong table. And sitting on the sofas was none other than the Zoomer family – George Zoomer, the dad; Lily Zoomer, the mom; and the kids, George, Jr. and Francine. Or, at least, the actors who played them. They weren't wearing their superhero costumes, just regular clothes, and they were playing gin rummy with a deck of cards.

"Where's our breakfast?" said the actor who played the dad. "We're starved."

"Yeah," said George, Jr. "And no more Zoomer Crunch cereal. We're sick of it!"

"Hey," Solly said, "I thought you guys were taking a break."

"Held prisoner, actually," said Lily Zoomer. "It'll be great publicity, right I.M.? We're going to be even more famous than before."

"And we're going to get raises," said Francine. "It's more like going on strike."

"How much do you make now?" Solly asked.

"A thousand dollars a week."

"Wow!"

"That's nothing," said George, Jr. "The kids on *Life with Andy* make three times as much."

"And they get to ride around in stretch limos," said Francine. "We just get ordinary limos. It isn't fair."

"Considering how much we have to put up with," said the dad. "Signing autographs. Making public appearances. Wearing those ridiculous costumes. We ought to have stretch limos with refrigerators and televisions in them."

"And our own personal assistants," added Lily.

"And bigger mansions."

"And more money."

"When are we going to get out of here, anyway? The TV doesn't even have cable."

Kaspar Snit grimaced. "Soon, soon. And Slouch will bring you breakfast. Come along, it's back upstairs for the rest of us."

"How about a Ping-Pong tournament first?" Solly said. "I'm great at Ping-Pong. I can beat anybody."

"You can't beat me," said the boy who played George, Jr.

"That's because you cheat," said Francine.

"I do not."

"Yes, you do. *Ouch!* Did you see that? He pinched me."

"Don't ask *me* to do something about it," said the woman who played Lily. "I'm not your real mother."

"I said upstairs." Kaspar Snit shooed us out of the room and closed the door. "Actors," he muttered, as we went back up.

So Kaspar Snit was holding the actors prisoner. But he was so clever that he had convinced them it was for their own advantage. They weren't trying to escape. They weren't even angry at him. It was weird to see them not acting anything like the Zoomer family. The dad wasn't kindly and wise, the mom wasn't patient and understanding, and the kids were anything but cheerful and cooperative. In fact, they were brats. They weren't a better family than ours; they weren't really a family at all.

10

A BRIEF HISTORY OF KASPAR SNIT'S LAST YEAR

We had to go back to our rooms while Slouch went to give breakfast to the actors. "Those actors," Mrs. Leer said, "are wrong to fool people. On strike, indeed."

"Mrs. Leer," I said, "do nannies ever go on strike?"

"Ah, my dear, I remember the great nanny strike of 1997 as if it were yesterday. I marched with my brothers and sisters, carrying a sign and singing proudly."

"Time for breakfast," said Slouch, appearing at the door.

"I'm not going," Solly said. "Besides, we already had breakfast."

"Then call it brunch. I thought you wanted to eat."

"Well, I'm tired of being ordered around."

"But Kaspar Snit insists that you come. Come on, don't make trouble." Slouch's voice rose anxiously. For the first time, I realized that he was afraid of Kaspar Snit too.

"Okay, but only if you give me a piggyback ride."

"Forget it."

"Then tell your boss that I'm staying in today."

"All right, but hurry up. And don't choke me."

A moment later, we were heading for the dining room.

"Stop kicking," Slouch said.

"I'm not kicking, I'm trying to hang on."

"Don't put your hands over my eyes!"

"Sorry."

We entered the dining room. Kaspar Snit was already seated, a giant canvas bag beside him. On the bag was stenciled the words OFFICIAL POST OFFICE USE ONLY and he was pulling an envelope from it. "Slouch!" he screamed. "What on earth are you doing? This isn't a day care. Put him down."

"I'll be glad to, boss. He's heavier than he looks."

"Sit down, all of you. And eat your cereal."

"Oh, good," Solly said. "Zoomer Crunch! Mom never lets us buy it at home. She says it's junk."

"Junk?" Kaspar Snit looked over. "What do you mean, junk?"

"Sugar, processed food, no fiber. Empty calories. She says you might just as well eat the box."

"Well, what do I care if it's healthy? What I care about is that it costs twenty-five cents to make and I can sell it for three dollars. Now, you'll excuse me if I look at my mail. Here's a lovely letter. I'll just read it aloud."

Dear Mr. Partankiss,

Here is all my allowance for the last two weeks. I was going to use it to buy my ma a birthday present, but I'm sending it to help the kids in Verulia build a new playground. I hope that you make more shows soon. I love *The Zoomers*. You must be a very wonderful person.

Signed,
Amy Lou Mittelhof, age nine.

"Isn't that sweet. Why, it warms my heart." Kaspar Snit poured the money from the envelope into his hand. "It'll be such a shame to disappoint Amy Lou," he said, examining a quarter.

"What do you mean, disappoint?" said Mrs. Leer. "Surely you are going to send that money to the people of Verulia. You have a responsibility to all the children who have sent it in."

Kaspar Snit stood up and put his hands on the table. "Madam, I have a responsibility only to myself. Send the money to the people of Verulia? Oh, it will go to Verulia all right, but not to the people. I shall use it to rebuild my fortress and equip a new army. I shall do grand, dastardly deeds. Once again my name will cause little children to shiver in their beds! I shall cast aside I.M. Partankiss and *The Zoomers*. I shall once more be Kaspar Snit!"

He banged his hand on the table, making our bowls jump.

"Please pass the milk," said Solly. "I need another bowl of Zoomer Crunch."

"Here you go," said Slouch.

"What are you doing?" Kaspar Snit said, snatching away the milk. "This is not the coffee shop of the Holiday Inn!"

I didn't want Kaspar Snit to keep getting mad at Solly, so I said, "I don't understand. The last thing we knew, you had escaped from the jail in Italy."

"Yes," said Mrs. Leer, "I remember reading about it in the newspaper. But how did you end up a television producer?"

"Ah," Kaspar Snit said, sitting down again. "At last, some interest in my remarkable comeback story. If you think it was easy, you are very wrong. I escaped from that Italian prison with nothing but the clothes on my back. You two imps might not understand, but I'm sure Mrs. Leer has seen more of the world. I have been made to suffer untold degradations these last months. In order to get out of that jail cell, I had to open the grate and crawl through a very smelly sewer. Picture that if you will, Mrs. Leer – me crawling through a sewer."

"Let me try," Mrs. Leer said. "Yes, I can imagine you in a sewer very well."

"Good. Next, I had to climb up a precarious drainpipe to the roof of the jail. There I found several dozen helium balloons tangled up. I used them to float away. Floating, let me tell you, is not the same as flying. You have no control. It is terrifying. I was pecked at by vicious seagulls. I sailed a good fifty miles before the balloons began to lose their buoyancy and I descended towards the ground. Down below me was a farm. Though I tried kicking my feet, I could not alter my course and landed in the mud of a pigsty. Imagine me, Mrs. Leer, wallowing in mud with snorting pigs!"

"I see it perfectly," said Mrs. Leer.

"I'm delighted. I managed to climb out and find the farmer on his tractor. He gave me a job as farmhand in exchange for room and meals. I had to shovel out the horse stables and clean the chicken coops. When I could take no more of such work, I set off on foot. I came to a port and managed to find a position as a dishwasher on a cruise ship. The sea was stormy and I was sick the entire time. I trust, Mrs. Leer, that you can see me in the hold of a ship, green with nausea and surrounded by stacks of dirty dishes."

"Wait a moment," Mrs. Leer said. "Yes, I've got it."

"I'm overjoyed. And all this time, madam, all this time, what did I think of? The Blande-Galinski family. I thought of their comfortable life and of how they had spoiled everything – all my years of hard work and devious planning. Most of all, I thought of Eleanor and Solly. I remembered how Eleanor refused my generous offer to let her join me in a life of dark deeds. Kids! Cute, adorable, obnoxious kids. The pride and joy of their parents. I hated kids more than anything else in the world."

"Well, thanks for the meal," Solly said. "I think I better be going."

"Stay where you are. At last the ship reached dry land. I considered returning to my youthful career as a pick-pocket and thief, but, in truth, I am not as nimble as I once was and I feared being recognized by the police. I decided that I had to keep within the law. I was forced to draw on my other talents. One of those talents, as you have no doubt noticed, madam, is charm."

"No, sir, I had not noticed," said Mrs. Leer.

"Well, take notice. I can charm just about anyone and get them to do what I want. That was how I took on Slouch here as my assistant. Slouch was pretending to be a porter, taking people's luggage off the ship. Only he would take it and not come back, wouldn't you, Slouch? I convinced him that he would get nowhere without some-one to show him the way."

"And you were right, boss. If it wasn't for you –"

"Be quiet, I'm telling the story. That first night, Slouch and I found a very unpleasant lodging house. Quite beneath me. In fact, it was so cold in our room that I had to put an old newspaper on top of the thin blanket to try and stay warm. Unable to sleep, I read the newspaper. It was a copy of *Variety*, a publication devoted to the enter-tainment business. I noticed a small advertisement calling for scripts for new television shows. Immediately I decided to write one. As you can also appreciate, madam, a facility with words is another of my talents."

"I have noticed you like the sound of your own voice," Mrs. Leer replied.

"And why should I not, when I speak so beautifully? But more than that, I realized that there was no better way to reach the children of this world than through the television screen. The very next day I wrote the first script of *The Zoomers*. It was accepted by the television studio and the rest, as they say, is history."

"But, Mr. Snit, I do not understand why you don't simply continue to write, direct, and produce your television show. You are successful, and no doubt very well paid. Do you not take any pleasure in living a respectable life?"

"I admit there is some satisfaction in being an artist, in seeing my words brought to life on the television screen each week. But do I take any pleasure in being respectable? No, I do not, madam. Having to be polite to studio executives? Telling the sensitive actors how wonderful they are? Flattering the heads of companies that advertise their products on my show? Making all those snot-nosed children watching my show happy? Of course not! I don't want to be a director of a mere television program when I can be the director of the world! Oh, how I've missed a life of evil deeds. And now Kaspar Snit is ready to return. There is just one thing, one thing more that I need."

"Some more Zoomer Crunch cereal?" asked Solly.

"Of course not. I wouldn't eat that junk. No," Kaspar Snit said, and he got up and walked around the table until he was beside my chair. Then he put his long icy fingers on my shoulder.

"You want to learn to fly?" I asked.

"Clever girl," Kaspar Snit said, pressing his fingers down hard.

11

A VERY LARGE CHICKEN

When brunch was over, Kaspar Snit told Slouch to take us back to our rooms on the set while he finished counting the money in the morning mailbag.

"I'm getting pretty tired of that room," Solly called, over his shoulder. "And that wallpaper! Bumblebees and butterflies – yuck. It's for a two-year-old."

But Kaspar Snit ignored him. He wanted to finish counting so that we could teach him to fly. He didn't say what he would do if we didn't teach him, but the menacing tone in his voice and the way he pressed his fingers into my shoulder were more than enough of a threat.

"This is a terrible dilemma," Mrs. Leer said, back in our rooms. "If you teach that awful man to fly, there's no telling what mischief he'll get up to. Swooping down on innocent people, causing fear and terror. It would be like giving a driver's license to a wolf."

"Mrs. Leer," Solly said, "a wolf couldn't drive even if it had a license. It wouldn't be able to reach the gas pedal."

"A very tall wolf. On the other hand, I can't allow you to put yourselves in danger by refusing. I wish that the dear, dreary Mr. Leer was here to offer his advice. He was a very sensible man. It made him a valuable asset to the Hindsight Insurance Company."

Solly climbed onto his bunk and started to polish his cracked goggles with the pillowcase. "Even if we wanted to teach him, we couldn't," Solly said. "We don't have the amulet."

"The what?"

"The silver amulet that Mom gave you," I said. "That's what gives us the power to fly. It's very ancient. It's belonged to our family for ages. You left it hanging on the picture by the bed. We don't have it, so we can't fly."

"You don't mean this, do you?" Mrs. Leer said. From underneath her blouse she pulled out a silver chain. And on the end of the chain was – the amulet!

"You have it!" I cried, jumping up from my bunk. "How did you get it?"

"I thought it would be safer here. But now if it is of some use to you –"

"Well, that's a pretty little bauble" came Kaspar Snit's rumbling voice. We all looked to see him standing in the doorway. He stepped over to Mrs. Leer and snatched the amulet from around her neck. "Very nice workmanship. Don't tell me; let me guess. It was a gift from your boring husband."

"Ah, yes, it was," Mrs. Leer said quickly. "And I'd be much obliged if you'd give it back."

She reached out, but Kaspar Snit pulled his hand away. He put the chain around his own neck so that the silver shone against the black velvet of the cape wrapped around him. "I think it goes rather well, don't you? How kind of you to offer it, madam. Now, all of you, out. It's time for that flying lesson. Go on, now."

He prodded me in the back and I went out the door, followed by Solly and Mrs. Leer. Kaspar Snit led us to the set of the outside of the Zoomers' house. Slouch was already there, leaning on the artificial tree and cutting his nails. I heard a noise and saw the pigeon perched on a low branch of the tree, preening its feathers.

"Slouch, stop that infernal clipping. And get rid of that pigeon. Shoot it with a bow and arrow."

"I don't have a bow and arrow, boss."

Kaspar Snit marched up to Slouch and swiped the nail clippers from his hand. He hurled them towards the pigeon, which fluttered up into the girders.

"You shouldn't do that," I said.

"I'll do whatever I like. I'll Kentucky fry that scrawny bird if I want to. Now, let's get started. There ought to be enough room here. This is a momentous day. I've been wanting to learn how to fly ever since you defeated me at my fortress."

"Yeah, that was pretty cool," Solly said, "the way Eleanor flew around you, wrapping you up with my elastic belt. It was bea-u-ti-ful."

"Yes, you defeated me then. But the thought of squeezing the secret of flying out of you," Kaspar Snit said, holding his fist in front of him and tightening it, "kept me going, even at the worst moments."

"Like when you were wallowing with the pigs?" I asked.

Kaspar Snit glared at me. I couldn't teach him. Even though the amulet was around his neck, I just couldn't. But I had to do something. I had to stall, to delay, at least until I figured out something else to do.

"Okay," I said, "Solly and I will teach you how to fly. But you have to do everything that we tell you."

"Eleanor, we can't!" Solly said.

"Solly, I'm your older sister," I said, looking him straight in the eye, trying to send him a message. "You have to listen to me. Now, in order to learn to fly, we'll need three things. First, a pillow. Second, a jar of honey. Third, breadcrumbs."

"Slouch, you heard her. Get a pillow from the set. And honey and breadcrumbs from the kitchen."

"Right, boss."

"My goodness," Mrs. Leer said. "What's all that for?"

"The initiation ceremony," I replied. "Solly and I had to do it, didn't we, Solly?"

Again I stared at my brother. He sure could be slow sometimes. But finally I saw his expression change as he started to understand. "Sure we did. You can't fly without taking the initiation ceremony. Everybody knows that."

Just then Slouch came back. "Here's the pillow and the honey. And the breadcrumbs."

"Good. Okay, Mr. Snit, time to take off your cape and your shirt."

"You can't be serious."

"Then don't learn to fly. I don't mind."

"All right," he mumbled, untying his cape. He folded it carefully and laid it on the porch step of the house set, placing the amulet on top. Then he took off his black satin shirt, revealing a sleeveless undershirt beneath. He had skinny arms.

"Not exactly working out at the gym, are you?" Solly said.

"Who has time these days?" Kaspar Snit snapped. "Now, let's get on with it."

"Fine," I said. Slouch was carrying the pillow under one arm, the jar of honey, and a cup of breadcrumbs. "Now, if Slouch will dribble honey all over your arms."

"You have got to be kidding."

"Nope. Not kidding at all."

"At least try not to make a mess, Slouch."

But it's pretty hard not to make a mess with honey. Slouch tipped the jar and the sweet and sticky liquid dribbled onto Kaspar Snit's arms. "It feels awful," he complained.

"Right," I said. "Now, Slouch, if you'll just tear a hole in the pillow for me. Good. Solly, help me to pull out the feathers. You know what to do with them."

"Sure," Solly said. "Can you, uh, remind me?"

"You have to stick them onto Kaspar Snit's arms."

"Oh, right!" Immediately he put his hand into the pillow and pulled out a handful of downy white feathers. He dropped them over Kaspar Snit's arm and, while a few drifted in the air, most of them stuck to the honey.

"This is truly disgusting," Kaspar Snit said.

"We must honor our bird ancestors," I said solemnly. "Go on, Solly, completely cover his arms."

"If I must. All done. You look like a new species of bird."

"The White-Tailed Snit. Which is just how you're supposed to look," I said, before Kaspar Snit had a chance to get angry. "Now, Slouch, pour those breadcrumbs onto the ground. You can do it just in front of the house. We need to attract that pigeon you scared away. Mrs. Leer, can you do any birdcalls?"

Mrs. Leer was staring in amazement at the sight of Kaspar Snit covered in feathers. "As a matter of fact, I do a rather realistic titwillow. The dear, dreary Mr. Leer used to admire it exceedingly."

"Good. It might help attract the pigeon."

Mrs. Leer cleared her throat, cupped her hands around her mouth, and made a series of high trills. From somewhere up above, I could hear wings thudding and, a moment later, I saw the pigeon fluttering between the girders. It found a lower perch and looked down at the breadcrumbs, tilting its head to one side and then the other. "I especially dislike pigeons," Kaspar Snit said, awkwardly holding out his feather-covered arms. We all watched as the pigeon flapped to the ground, skittering on its scaly feet. It looked at us a moment, pecked at the crumbs, and looked at us again before pecking some more.

"It's now or never," I said. "You have to kneel down. Solly and I will be on either side of you."

"I do not kneel for anything," Kaspar Snit said.

"Then you can't fly. Okay, who wants to play tag instead?"

"All right, all right. This is humiliating." He knelt down on the ground. I signaled Solly to take a position on one side of him while I knelt on the other.

"Repeat after me," I said. "O great bird."

"You want me to speak to a miserable pigeon?"

"You're not cooperating."

"All right. O great bird."

"Master of flight," I said.

"Master of flight."

"King of the air."

"King of the hair."

"I said *air*."

"Sorry. King of the air."

"It's my turn," Solly said. And then louder, "Share with me your great power."

"Share with me your great power."

"Let me be one with the eagle, the rooster, the chickadee, and the penguin."

I hissed at Solly, "Penguins can't fly!"

"Cancel the penguin," Solly said. Then he stood up. I stood up. Kaspar Snit groaned and stood up. Solly lifted one foot. I lifted one foot. Kaspar Snit lifted one foot. Now I began to flap my arms. Solly flapped his and, when Kaspar Snit started, feathers flew everywhere. Solly began to chirp loudly. I started to peep-peep. Kaspar Snit began to caw. Behind us, Slouch quacked like a duck.

The pigeon lifted its head and looked at us. "Do you feel it?" I asked. "Do you feel your inner bird power?"

"I feel it!" Kaspar Snit cried. "I feel it!"

"Now you must use that power. You must find a high place and jump!"

"Yes, yes! I must fly, I must fly!"

Kaspar Snit began running about, wildly flapping his arms. He spotted the artificial tree, rushed over to it, and climbed into its low branches, cawing all the while. He inched his way up to a wide branch and stood on it.

Slouch shouted, "Do it, boss, do it! Fly!"

"O great birds of the world, I join you!"

He jumped.

Fortunately there was a pile of fake leaves near the bottom of the tree. It softened Kaspar Snit's fall. Still, he hit the ground pretty hard and cried out in pain. "My knee! My bad knee!" He pushed himself to a sitting position, and rubbed his leg.

Slouch said, "I saw you fly, boss. I did! A little, anyway."

"I did not fly, you imbecile. I've been tricked." He made a face, moving his mouth around, and then, with two fingers, pulled a feather out from between his lips. "I've been made a fool of by a couple of smarty-pants kids. And they're going to pay for it. Where are my clothes?"

We all looked over to the neatly folded cape and shirt and saw that the pigeon was standing on them. Underneath the pigeon was a runny white glop. "Oh, great. Just look at that," Kaspar Snit said, getting up. "That revolting bird has pooped on my shirt. I'm going to ring its neck!"

The pigeon pecked at a button on Kaspar Snit's shirt. Then it saw the shiny amulet and picked up the delicate chain in its beak. Kaspar Snit lunged towards it and the bird flapped into the air, holding the amulet.

"Oh, no!" I cried. "The amulet. Solly, get it!"

Solly ran towards the pigeon and jumped up, but the bird flew out of his grasp and kept going until it was high up in the girders. Still it kept going and, for a moment, it was visible in the center of the blue circle of sky that was the hole in the peak. And then it was gone. It had flown outside.

When I looked down again, I saw Kaspar Snit staring at me. "I'll show you the consequences of toying with Kaspar Snit." He strode over to me and reached out his two hands, with their long cold fingers. I would have screamed, except that I couldn't. I was frozen with fear. I closed my eyes.

"Unhand that girl!" The voice came from above.

"Who in the blazes is that?" growled Kaspar Snit. I felt him step away and, when I opened my eyes, I saw him squinting up towards the mountain's peak. I looked too, but at first all I could see were the girders arching up to the hole that showed the sky. Then suddenly I saw something swoop down inside the peak. *Was it a . . . a . . . superhero?*

It was a man in a stretchy yellow leotard, black boots, a cape, and some sort of helmet on his head.

"My goodness," said Mrs. Leer. "I've never had quite this much adventure on a job before."

"Solly," I said, "do you know which superhero this is?"

"I'm thinking," he said, looking up. "It might be Asteroid Man. No, it's Lightning Flash. Or maybe the Liberator. Well, it's somebody!"

Whoever it was, he had a very strange way of flying. It looked more like running through the air, or maybe swinging, the way he went back and forth, a little lower each time.

"Let those people go!" the superhero shouted down. "The law will go easier on you if you give yourself up."

"Forgive me if I don't oblige you," Kaspar Snit said. "Exactly which superhero are you, anyway?"

"Why I'm . . . I'm . . . Banana Man!"

"Banana Man? That's pathetic. And who was your mother, Fruit Basket?"

"It's not my fault that all the good names were taken. And since we're asking questions, why are you covered in feathers?"

"Tell him it's a fashion statement," said Solly.

"It's a fashion statement," repeated Kaspar Snit. "No, it isn't. Never you mind, Peel Man."

"It's Banana Man. Now this is your last warning. Give up now. If I have to . . . *whoa!*"

Banana Man looked like he was in trouble. At least, I didn't think he meant to be spinning in circles. He was low enough now that I could see what it said on the back of his cape – RIZNIK MAKES THE CRUNCHIEST PICKLES.

Wait a minute, we had a towel like that at home.

Suddenly, Banana Man began to jerk up and down. "I think I'm going to be sick."

"Having a little trouble?" Kaspar Snit asked.

"It's nothing. Just a little stabilization problem. I'll get it right in a minute." He halted in midair, slowly turned upside down, and moved downwards in a series of small jerks. Only when he was lying on the ground could I see that he was wearing a hockey helmet. And that there was a wire attached to him.

Kaspar Snit strode up and pulled the helmet off.

"Dad!" Solly cried, running towards him. I ran too, and we both hugged him even before he could unclip the wire and get up.

"Hi, kids," he said, looking rather embarrassed.

"Hey, Dad, did you have a good time in Italy?"

"Lovely, thank you. Of course, we missed you both terribly."

"This is all very chummy," Kaspar Snit said. "But if you don't mind, I have some evil to attend to. No doubt it was your delightful wife, Daisy, controlling the wire from above. If she would be so kind as to join us."

We all looked up. And there, in the light of the opening, I could just make out my mother's face. "Hi, Eleanor. Hi, Solly," she said, waving. "I'll be right down."

12

A LETTER TO THE COMMITTEE

It turned out that Mom and Dad had been phoning us from Italy and, getting no answer, started to worry. They took an earlier flight home and, finding the house empty, had immediately gone to the police. The same desk sergeant who we had spoken to told them of our crazy story about Solly being held captive in Misery Mountain. That was when they realized that Kaspar Snit was up to no good. Mom couldn't fly – the markings on her hand had faded away – so Dad had come up with the plan of pretending he could. He thought the element of surprise would cause Kaspar Snit to let us go.

"I guess I wanted to be the big hero, even if I can't fly," Dad said, shaking his head at himself as he sat on the lower bunk. "I thought that Kaspar Snit would surrender."

"I'm sorry, Manfred," Mom said. "That wire was just too hard to control."

"Well, if nothing else, I have a new appreciation for real flying."

I sat down beside him and he took my hand. "Dad," I said, "why do you think that you're the only one in the family who can't fly?"

"I'm not sure, Eleanor. Maybe I'm just a feet-on-the-ground sort of person."

"You know what I think?" I said. "It's because, deep down, you don't think a person really ought to fly."

My dad sighed.

"Meanwhile," Mom said, "we're stuck here and we don't know what Kaspar Snit is going to do with us."

"After he gets all the feathers off, you mean," Solly said.

"You kids," Dad chuckled. "Making him act like a bird."

"You know what's really bad?" I said. "How Mrs. Leer feels."

Mrs. Leer had gone into her own room, even though my parents asked her to stay with us. She had said that we needed time alone as a family, but I knew it was because she blamed herself for our capture.

"You're right, Eleanor," Mom said. "Let's see if we can get her to join us."

We went to the door and Mom knocked lightly. "Mrs. Leer? We'd love to have your company."

"I'm fine where I am, thank you. Unless, of course, you require my services."

"Yes, we need you."

Mrs. Leer came into our room.

"First," Mom said, "you can keep us company. And second, you can give me back the amulet that I asked you to wear for safekeeping. It's going to get us out of here."

Solly and I looked at each other. Mrs. Leer said, "I'm afraid it is another of my failures. You asked me to keep it safe and I did not."

"It wasn't your fault," Solly said. "Kaspar Snit made you give it to him."

"Kaspar Snit has the amulet?" Dad said.

"No, a pigeon flew off with it," I answered. "We don't know where it went."

"We saw a pigeon," Mom said. "It flew out of the hole just as I was going to lower your father down. It was carrying something shiny."

"Then it's really gone," I said. "We don't have the amulet anymore."

"That means no more flying," said Solly. "Not ever."

Solly was right. There would be no more flying without the amulet. I hadn't had a moment to think about it. A life without flying, I could hardly imagine it. Flying was the one thing that always lifted my spirits, no matter how down I felt. Flying wasn't just something I did for fun; it was part of who I was. It was part of what made me Eleanor. And now what would I do?

"What a delightful scene. The Blande family reunited."

It was Kaspar Snit. He was standing in our doorway, wearing his grim smile. He was dressed in his cape again and his black hair was wet and slicked back. The feathers were gone.

"All right, Snit," my father said. "The game is over. It's time for you to let us go."

"Let you go? Why, the fun is only beginning. So far, your children have failed to teach me to fly. But I don't give up that easily. I believe that Daisy will be a far better instructor. After all, Daisy, you wouldn't want anything to happen to your husband and children, would you?"

"But I can't teach you," Mom said.

"Oh, but I think you can."

"I can't teach you because I can't fly anymore. And neither can the kids."

"Can't fly? What do you mean?"

"The amulet is gone," I said.

"Amulet? You mean that silver piece that I took from the nanny?"

"Yes," Mom said. "That's what gave us the power to fly. But the pigeon flew away with it."

"I do believe you're telling the truth. I knew there was something special about that necklace. Rats!" Kaspar Snit smacked his hand on the wall, making it shake. "But, wait a minute, this is almost as good. I won't be able to fly, but you can't either."

"That's right," Mom said.

"So the Blandes have lost their specialness. They're just ordinary folk, like everyone else. What a pity. Of course this will mean a change of plans for me. I'll have to do evil the old-fashioned way. And I know just how I'm going to start – by showing children everywhere what suckers they are. They'll soon learn that they can't trust anybody."

"How do you intend to do that?" Manfred asked.

"I don't suppose you've ever watched a live television show? Well, you're in for a treat. Slouch will come for you when everything is ready."

He turned and walked away, but we could still hear his laughter.

All right, I thought as I lay back on my bunk and stared at the bottom of the mattress above me. *So I couldn't fly anymore. It wasn't the end of the world, was it?*

It was my dad who told me that I sometimes looked at things the wrong way, that I saw the negative and not the positive. If I wasn't going to fly anymore, then I would have to find something – something more normal – that I liked as much, that made me feel just as good.

I couldn't think of anything.

Surely there was something. *Hang gliding?* But holding on to a kite while being pulled by a boat sounded scary to me, and kind of dumb.

High-wire walking? Sumo wrestling? Rock climbing? Spelunking?

I sighed. Nothing that I could think of sounded right. But maybe that only meant that I had to make up something never tried before. A new sport. Yes, that was it. I thought hard.

Underwater bowling?

Oh, brother. Surely I could do better than that.

Ballet tennis?

Not likely.

Blindfolded downhill skiing? Booster-rocket skateboarding? Maybe there was nothing that could replace flying, not for me.

A knock made me look up. It was Mrs. Leer. "Are you busy?" she said to my parents.

"No, no, please come in," said Mom.

Mrs. Leer stepped into our room. She looked very grim. "Perhaps," she said, "this is a good time to show you what I have been doing in my room. Mr. Blande, Ms. Galinski, I would appreciate it if you would read this letter. Since it is likely that the recipients will contact you, I think it best that you know about it beforehand."

My parents took it from her hand. At first, they weren't going to let me read it too, but Mrs. Leer said that she did not wish to hide anything. I squeezed between them and read it.

To the International Union of Extraordinary Caregivers
North American Headquarters
318 Betty Anne Lane
Winnipeg, Manitoba

Dear Members of the Disciplinary Committee,

As you are aware, I have been a member in good standing of our worthy organization for the past eighteen years. I have tried to maintain the highest standards of our profession and, with all humility, I believe that I have upheld those standards to the letter. It is therefore with heavy regret that I submit my resignation.

The reason is as follows. In my most recent position (see client file number 147-B), I have violated regulation 143, subsection D, which states

No nanny shall allow her charges to be enticed, kidnapped, bundled off, carried away, grabbed, shanghaied, spirited away, or snatched; or to be held hostage, impounded, detained, shut in, confined, or in any other manner removed and kept from her direct supervision.

I make no excuses, nor offer extenuating circumstances. I take full responsibility. Please find enclosed my membership card, my NANNY OF THE YEAR citation, and my discount card from the Sensible Clothing Company.

Although I shall no longer be a member of the I.U.E.C., I hope that I will be allowed to continue my subscription to the magazine *Nanny!* In this way, I hope to keep up on the progress and issues of my former calling. At the risk of sentimentality, may I say that, although I shall no longer be practising, in my heart I shall always remain a nanny.

Yours respectfully,
Lucretia Leer

Mrs. Leer said it was the hardest letter that she had ever written. My parents objected strenuously to it, trying to convince her that she wasn't at fault and that she was too good a nanny to quit the profession.

"Fine words, Mr. Blande and Ms. Galinski, but they will do no good. The rule and the penalty are very clear. My career must come to an ignoble end."

Mrs. Leer looked sad, but determined. My parents could think of nothing to say. Finally, Solly piped up.

"Is your name really Lucretia?"

Mrs. Leer nodded. Then she went into her room and, a moment later, we heard the mournful sound of her tin whistle.

"'The Last Farewell,'" said Dad quietly. "Good choice."

13

A TOAST AND AN OFFER

The only box among the stacked shelves in the Zoomer kids' bedroom with anything in it was a checkers game. Naturally, Solly found it. I didn't think checkers was very exciting, but there was nothing else to do, so Solly and I were playing. In fact, we'd been playing for about two hours and I'd beaten him seven times. Solly wasn't one to get discouraged, though. "I'm refining my strategy," he said. "As soon as I get it right, I'll be unbeatable."

"If you say so," I yawned, jumping over three of his pieces.

"Hey, checkers – my favorite game. Can I play?" It was Slouch standing in the doorway.

"Eleanor's pretty good," Solly said.

"Nobody beats the Slouch. Move over, kid, and let a master show you how it's done."

Solly moved over and Slouch sat down. My parents didn't look too pleased to have Kaspar Snit's assistant in the room, but they didn't say anything.

"How about we make it interesting? Say, a dollar a game?"

"I don't have a dollar," I said.

"Okay, ten cents."

"There will be no gambling," Dad said.

"All right, spoilsport. I'll go first," Slouch said. Then he sat staring at the board and scratching his chin for a good two minutes. Finally, he moved. I moved. He thought, put a finger on a piece, moved it forward and then back. And so it went, until, one by one, I picked his pieces off the board.

"I must be having an off day," Slouch said, rubbing his head. "Let's do best two-out-of-three."

"What is going on here?"

It was Kaspar Snit.

"We're just playing checkers, boss. Want a game?"

"No, I don't want a silly game. It's times like this that I miss my warrior army most. Come along, all of you. We're going to have a little celebration."

Once again, we were marched onto the set before the Zoomers' house. This time there was a little table with a bottle of champagne and a single glass on it, and beside the table, an enormous pile of money – bills and coins, piled twice as high as Kaspar Snit himself. Also beside the table was a small mailbag. "Slouch," he said, "turn over the mailbag."

"Sure thing, boss."

When he tipped the canvas bag over, a single envelope fell out. "What have we here?" Kaspar Snit said. He picked up the envelope and slit it open with the long nail of his thumb. He pulled out the blue sheet of paper. "Let me read it," he said. "No, better still, let Eleanor read it out loud."

He held out the blue paper. I took it and saw that the letter was printed in crayon, the letters crooked. There were stickers on the paper, too – a dog, a smiley face, and a star. Definitely a little kid's letter. "Go on, read it," Kaspar said, with an edge in his voice. So I did.

Dear Mr. Partankiss,

My name is Davey Golightly. I am seven years old. Do you have any pets? I don't. Dogs and cats make me sneeze. I was saving up my allowance to buy a hairless guinea pig. But instead, I am sending my money to you to give to the people of Verulia. I love *The Zoomers*. I wish I was part of the Zoomer family. I am an only child. I want to be like you when I grow up.

From your Number One Fan,
Davey Golightly

I finished reading and looked up. "The poor kid," said my dad.

"Yes, how touching," Kaspar Snit said. "Getting a letter like that ought to be reward enough for the work I've done. But, you know what? It isn't. And, oh look, there's something else in the envelope."

Kaspar Snit tipped the envelope over. From it poured silver coins and copper pennies. "Let me see. Two dollars . . . two seventy-five . . . three. A total of three dollars and twenty-six cents. If I add that to the amount that has already come in, that makes – why, that makes *one million dollars*. It looks like I've really hit the jackpot, doesn't it? With a million dollars I can rebuild my fortress, recruit a new army, and do an awful lot of evil. Yes, this does call for a toast."

Kaspar Snit picked up the bottle of champagne. He popped the cork and filled the glass. He raised the glass and gave us that awful smile – a smile that revealed no happiness, only an ugly sort of pleasure. "Now, who shall I make this toast to? I know, to all the *Zoomer* fans who will watch television tonight. May their little hearts break!" He drank the champagne in one gulp.

"Stealing money from all those kids," said my mother. "Kids who have watched your show. It's about the most cynical act I've ever seen. I can't imagine what you're going to do on television tonight that can be worse."

"I'll tell you what's worse. Tonight is going to be the very last episode of *The Zoomers*. I've told the television network that we are going on the air, live, at seven o'clock. They've already announced it in the newspapers and on the radio. Millions of kids will tune in, hoping to see their favorite show. And you know what they will see instead? Me. Yes, me, surrounded by all this money they've sent in. And you know what I'm going to tell them? That they've been duped! That they're a bunch of suckers. I'm going to announce my real identity – Kaspar Snit, evil genius! And then – *poof!* – I'm going to disappear. At least until my next performance. Meanwhile, I'll leave behind millions of disappointed and disillusioned kiddy hearts. Do you know what they'll learn from seeing me? That they can't trust anybody. That they should never believe what they're told. That life is a scam, a game where the cheater always wins. Hold on to your money, kids: Don't try to be generous, don't try to help other people. Because being good to others is for losers."

Kaspar Snit's voice had grown louder and louder until he stood, arms raised triumphantly, before us. We all just stared at him, until finally Mrs. Leer spoke.

"Rest assured, Mr. Snit, that your actions will be highly disapproved of by the International Union of Extraordinary Caregivers. I shouldn't be surprised if you were named this year's Worst Influence on Children."

"What an honor," Kaspar Snit said. "Does it come with a trophy? And now, if you wouldn't mind going back to your rooms, Slouch and I have a television show to prepare. Slouch, I want you to set up a camera facing the front of the house set. I'll be sitting in the rocking chair beside all that money. It'll be so quaint, don't you think?"

We all turned to go, when Kaspar Snit said, "Eleanor, wait. Why don't you stay? I'm sure you'll find this very interesting."

"Thanks, but no thanks."

"I said that you should stay."

"All right."

"What do you want with Eleanor?" Mom said, putting her arms around me.

"Just a little chat. She'll join you soon. I give you my word."

Mom leaned down. "Don't trust anything he says," she whispered into my ear. I watched her join Dad, Mrs. Leer, and Solly, as they went back to the rooms. Slouch was moving a big camera that was mounted on a three-legged stand with wheels. The camera had a light on top and cables that connected to a nearby panel. He looked through the viewfinder and adjusted the lens.

"It's all set up, boss."

"Good. Go and check on our actors, will you? We don't want them to get too restless."

"Okay, boss."

Slouch opened the door in the tree and disappeared.

"What are you going to do with the actors after your show tonight?" I asked.

"I'm going to let them go," Kaspar Snit said. "They're more trouble than you can imagine. Always whining about something. Of course, it'll be a bit of a surprise to them to find out that, instead of raises, they're actually being fired. But I'm sure they can find jobs as waiters."

"And what about me and my family? And Mrs. Leer?"

"Hmm. That's an excellent question. I haven't quite decided. But I'm thinking of holding on to you all. I'm sure you'll be useful somehow."

"We won't be useful. We'll just be in the way. You should let us go too."

"Well, Eleanor, I appreciate the suggestion. But it really won't do. However, I'm a reasonable man. Why don't I make a counteroffer? I'll let them go if you stay."

"Me?"

"Yes, you. Remember when I was holding you and your family in the dungeon of my fortress? You got out one night and found me among the fountains I had stolen. I asked you then to join me, to become my assistant. But you refused. If anything, I am *more* certain that you would make an excellent sidekick. You are a most resourceful girl. And devious, too, when you want to be. Just look at how you got me to cover myself in feathers. Really, it was masterful. With the right attitude, you could do a great deal of mischief. And worse."

"But you've got Slouch."

"That nitwit? He couldn't get an olive out of a jar. No, Slouch will find himself in a very different situation once I've got my warrior army back. Open your mind to the possibility, Eleanor. Just think of what we could achieve together. Look at me. I'm just as misunderstood, just as alone as I was then. Do you think that evil geniuses don't get lonely? That they don't want someone to talk to, someone to share the good times and the bad? When I asked you the first time, you were too young. But now you are a year older. Almost a teenager. I'm sure there are times when you are angry at your parents, when they still treat you as if you were a kid. When you wish that you didn't have to listen to them."

"I guess so."

"And I bet there are all kinds of things you want to have and they won't let you have."

"Well, sure."

"And I bet you don't always want to be good, either. I bet you don't always want to do your homework and help clear the table after dinner and be nice to your brother. I bet there are times when you'd rather be selfish and mean."

I didn't want to admit it, but I said, "Sometimes."

"If you join forces with me, Eleanor, you'll be able to do whatever you want. You'll be able to *have* whatever you want. You can be selfish and mean and I won't get mad. Why, I'll praise you for it. I'll reward you for it! And, with you at my side, I'll be able to accomplish so much more. You see, I've developed a taste for influencing the kids of the world. Influencing them for the worse, I mean. After all, what better way to get at parents – people like your own mother and father – than to turn their children into selfish, miserable, troublemaking little brats? I'm an adult, but you're still a kid. Just think of how you, as my sidekick, could be a role model for kids. Seeing you succeed through treachery, deceit, and plain nastiness will do more harm than I ever could. What do you say, Eleanor? Are you ready now? Will you join me? And, oh, yes. I'd let your family go."

"You'd let them go?"

"Right after the broadcast. You come with me, and they can walk out of this glue-and-paper mountain."

I looked down at my feet. For the first time I realized that I had put on different-colored socks, one blue and one red. If I stayed with Kaspar Snit, he'd probably want me to wear black socks and black everything else. But I had to save my family.

"All right," I said. "But please, don't tell my parents right now. It'll only be a secret until we leave."

"Fine," Kaspar Snit said. Slowly his mouth curled into a grin. "It'll be our little secret, partner."

14

THE LAST PROGRAM

Back in our room, Mrs. Leer and the family were trying to come up with plans of their own. "What if I put chewing gum on my hands and feet that is so sticky, I could climb up the inside of the mountain and get out?" Solly said.

"I could jump on top of Kaspar Snit and cover his eyes with my hands," Dad offered.

"With your bad back?" Mom said. "Don't even think about it. And you, Solly, don't even try. Maybe I can reason with him."

"Hello? Have you actually been listening to him?" Dad said.

"Perhaps I could remind him of his own childhood," Mrs. Leer suggested. "He might be able to relate to all those children out there."

All of their ideas sounded pretty hopeless to me, but I didn't say anything. A little while later, Slouch brought us dinner – canned spaghetti with pineapple slices and sardines – and even Solly didn't find it very appetizing.

"I feel bad for all those kids," my dad said. "Finding out that they've been duped. That they opened their hearts and sent in their money, only to have it stolen. Kaspar Snit's right – they'll never trust anyone again."

"Even an extraordinary nanny won't be able to undo that sort of harm," Mrs. Leer said. "Ah, it is a sad day."

"Yes," murmured my mom. It was a sad day, worse than they even knew. If only I could fly, but that pigeon must be miles away by now. The amulet was probably decorating some nice pigeon nest high up in a tree.

Absentmindedly, I opened my hand to see if there was anything left of the markings on my palm. What I saw made me look closer, for there was a very thin violet outline of the moon and three stars. Not an outline with gaps here and there like before, but complete and unbroken, thin but perfect. The remaining spaces must have filled in the last time that I took an impression with the amulet. *What did it mean?* I wondered. *Why didn't the others have it and what was the good of just an outline?*

Slowly I stood up. I went to the corner of the room and looked at the others. Mom returned my gaze and smiled wistfully, then she put her head down. Dad, Solly, and Mrs. Leer were staring into their bowls. For an experiment, I put my hands at my side, cocked at thirty degrees, and closed my eyes.

My feet fluttered up from the ground.

"Eleanor?"

I opened my eyes. "Yes, Mom?"

"What are you doing, honey?"

"Oh, nothing. Just feeling restless, I guess."

"I know the food tastes pretty bad, but I think you should eat some more. We all need our strength."

"All right." I went back to my bowl, jittery with excitement. My feet had risen just a little from the ground. When I looked up again, I saw Mrs. Leer gazing at me.

"My dear," she said, under her breath. "Did I see what I thought I saw?"

"I think so," I answered.

We were interrupted by Kaspar Snit's voice. "It's showtime, folks." He was staring at me with a secret glint in his eye. "I want all of you to witness this landmark event. All those unhappy children! It's going to be marvelous. Hurry up now, we go on the air in six minutes!"

"Excuse me if I do not come," said Mrs. Leer. "I have no wish to witness such a mean-spirited act. You are nothing but a bully."

"You are right – I am a bully. And you have no choice. Now come along, everyone; hop to it!"

We didn't hop to it, but we did come, dragging our feet down the corridor. There was a row of chairs set up behind the camera and Kaspar Snit directed us to sit down. Slouch, wearing earphones, was checking the camera one last time, waiting for Kaspar Snit to take his place on the porch. To the side was a television – on, but with the sound turned off – and I could see the woman reporter with the puffy hair speaking into a microphone. No doubt she was telling the viewers about the upcoming announcement from I.M. Partankiss.

"Ten seconds!" Slouch called. "Nine . . . eight . . . six. . . ."

"You missed seven!" Solly called.

"Darn. I always miss seven. Three . . . two . . . one. We're on the air!"

The light on top of the camera turned green. Kaspar Snit, in his sunglasses and black beret, smiled into the lens. I turned and saw him on the television screen and then looked back at the real person. "Good evening, children everywhere. Thank you for tuning into *The Zoomers*. I'm sorry to say that, once again, there will be no program. In fact, there will never be another episode of *The Zoomers*. Don't think it's because all of you fans did not send enough money for Verulia. No, in fact, I have a tidy one million dollars, thanks to all of you. How generous of you to send your nickels and dimes. What an act of faith and goodwill and generosity it was. Well, I'm sorry to tell you that – *it was all for nothing!*"

Kaspar Snit stood up, removed his beret and his glasses, and stepped closer to the camera. "Well, not for nothing. Actually, it was all for little old me. That's right, children, you have wasted your precious pennies. You see, I.M. Partankiss is not my real name at all. It's . . . *Kaspar Snit*! That's right – Kaspar Snit, evil genius. Are you frightened?

Are you shivering? Well, you should be. I have your money and I am keeping it all for myself. I tricked you. I lied to you. I stole from you. That, dear children, is a lesson that you should thank me for. Don't trust people. Don't be generous. Don't be hopeful. Or else the world will pick your pockets and make a dope out of you!"

Kaspar Snit took yet another step closer to the camera. On the television screen, his face looked huge and threatening. "What did you think, you ridiculous babies? That you can make the world a better place? That there are superheroes who will protect you from meanies like me? There aren't any. That people can fly? They can't. Get real. *Grow up!* And now, I'm going to take all the lovely money that you've sent and do even more evil deeds, until I am truly the greatest evil genius in the history of the world! So you'd better look out. You'd better check under your bed tonight, and in your closet, and outside your window, because you never know. Somebody might be lurking there. Somebody named . . . Kaspar Snit!" He took a step back, crossed his arms with satisfaction, and stared hard into the camera.

I could feel Mrs. Leer trembling beside me. "He can't do this," she muttered. "We must do something, we must."

"You're right, Mrs. Leer, but what?" whispered my dad.

"I'll show you what," Mrs. Leer said, with gritty determination. My mother gasped as Mrs. Leer got up from her chair and strode right up to Kaspar Snit. I could see her on the television monitor, which meant that millions of people were seeing her on their screens at home.

"Children," Mrs. Leer said. "Don't listen to this nasty man. What he says isn't true. Why, in fact, nothing he says is true."

Kaspar Snit gave Mrs. Leer his most insulting smirk. "Oh, really?" he said. "You mean the world *is* a better place because all of these kids gave me their money? The next thing you're going to tell me is, people can really fly."

"As a matter of fact, they can. And I know just the person to demonstrate."

Mrs. Leer pointed her finger.

She pointed her finger at *me*.

"Come on, dear, don't be shy."

"What's this about?" said Kaspar Snit.

I got up. "Eleanor," Mom whispered. "Put on Solly's goggles."

Solly handed them to me and I put them on. I walked as stiffly as a robot to Mrs. Leer. When I looked over, I could see myself on the monitor. The crack in the goggles looked pretty goofy, but maybe people wouldn't recognize who I was.

"Slouch, turn off the camera," Kaspar Snit commanded.

"Right, boss."

Solly got up. I saw him take his rat, G.W., out of the pocket in his cape, kiss him on the nose, and place him on Slouch's shoulder.

"What's that?" Slouch said.

"Just a rat," Solly said.

"A . . . *rat*?"

Slouch turned his head to see, but G.W. scampered to his other shoulder.

"Yikes, get it off me!" Slouch let go of the camera. It swung down so that, on the monitor, I could see Kaspar Snit's black boots. Slouch squirmed as G.W. worked his way down his back. "I hate rodents!" he cried, dancing around.

Solly dragged a chair over to the camera and stood on it so that he could look through the viewfinder. He pointed it at me.

"Okay, sis," he said. "I got you covered. Show your stuff."

"This television show is over," Kaspar Snit snarled.

"No, it isn't," I said. I closed my eyes, put my hands in position, and took a deep breath to calm down. I could feel myself lift into the air. When I opened my eyes again, I was hovering over the set, just below the stage lights. *The outline on my hand worked!* I could still fly. Looking down at the monitor, I saw myself from below. I looked pretty cool.

"Watch this!" I said, swooping down and then up again.

"This is great!" Solly cried. "Do something else."

"Okay. Ah, hi, there, TV land."

"What are you doing?" Kaspar Snit shouted from below. "Get down!" He jumped up, trying to grab hold of my foot, but I rose higher just in time. Solly caught it on the camera, making Kaspar Snit look pretty silly.

"I guess all you kids watching are wondering what's going on," I said, looking into the lens. "I just want you to know that what Kaspar Snit said is wrong. I mean, look at me. He said people can't fly. But I'm flying, aren't I? And if I can, then the other things he said can't be true either."

To make my point, and to show that I wasn't attached to any wires, I did a somersault in the air. To be honest, Solly was better at them then me – I always got dizzy – but I did all right. "I want to thank all of you for sending in your money," I said. "You were great to send it in. You were amazing. I want to assure you that Kaspar Snit isn't going to get it. No, we're going to make sure that those people in Verulia use it to rebuild their homes and schools and hospitals, just like you wanted."

"That's right!" shouted Solly, from behind the camera. "And also their candy stores, their waterslides, and their rock-climbing walls."

I wasn't sure that Verulia had waterslides, but I let it slide. Actually, I wasn't quite sure how we were going to get the money from Kaspar Snit, but I decided to figure that out later. "So I just want to say that you shouldn't give up caring about other people. I mean, if someone like me can fly, then anything is possible, right?"

I felt something tug on my foot. Looking down, I saw that Kaspar Snit had made a lasso with an electrical cord and thrown it around my ankle. "Come down from there, you miserable little brat!" He pulled so hard that I came crashing down on top of him.

"*Ouch!* Get off me!"

At that moment, Mom and Dad rushed up and held Kaspar Snit down. Then Mrs. Leer rushed forward and used the electrical cord to tie up Kaspar Snit's hands.

"Regulation 306-B," Mrs. Leer said. "'A nanny must know all major sailor's knots.' There, that ought to hold him. Would you children watching on the television kindly call the police and send them to Partankiss Productions?"

My parents held Kaspar Snit down by sitting on him as he struggled in the cords.

"Let's have something special for dinner tonight," Mom said.

"Good idea, darling."

"Mrs. Leer," I whispered, "we need some music. Play your tin whistle."

"Certainly," Mrs. Leer said, taking it out of her pocket. "How about a little 'Fisher's Hornpipe'?"

As she began to play, I spoke into the camera: "Well, thanks for tuning in. And remember, kids, you might not be able to fly, but everybody can be good at something. It just takes practise. Well, I guess that's about all. Good night and good luck."

I smiled and waved. The camera kept on me. "Solly," I whispered, "turn it off."

"Oh, sorry," said Solly. The light on top of the camera went red.

15

THE M.F.G.

Five minutes after we went off the air, there was a knock on the door leading into Misery Mountain. My father opened it to find two police officers, a man and a woman. The man was the same officer who Mrs. Leer and I had spoken to in the police station.

"Excuse me," the policewoman said. "We received a telephone call."

"Actually," said the policeman, looking past my father at me, "we received about three thousand telephone calls."

"Then the switchboard broke down," added the policewoman. "We understand that you have Kaspar Snit on the premises. He's wanted for escaping from jail, kidnapping, fraud, and a dozen other charges."

"I should have listened to your daughter," the officer said.

"I learned that lesson a long time ago," my father said. "Come this way."

The police found Kaspar Snit bound up with the electrical cord. "Well, well," said the officer from the desk. "A little tied up today, are you, Mr. Snit?"

Kaspar Snit glared at him. "You're a regular comedian," he grumbled.

"And what is that – electrical cord? Why, that's shocking. Get it? Electrical cord – shocking?"

"I get it. Now, will you please arrest me? It's better than having to listen to your jokes."

"Excuse me, officers," Dad said. "But I think we should look for Kaspar Snit's accomplice, Slouch."

"Good idea," said the woman officer. "Any idea where he's gone?"

"I know where he is," Solly said. "He's right over there. G.W. is watching him."

We looked to where Solly was pointing. There was Slouch, pressed against a corner of the studio, trembling with fear. On the ground in front of him, about the size of a kid's running shoe, was G.W., bristling up his fur and making squeaking noises whenever Slouch moved.

"Either G.W. is the world's first guard-rat," said Solly, "or Slouch has cookies in his pocket."

Slouch looked embarrassed. "Chocolate chip," he admitted.

Solly picked up G.W., kissed him on the nose, gave him a piece of chocolate-chip cookie from Slouch, and slipped him back into his cape pocket.

The police officers led the actors out of the basement and Mom asked them to help us put all the money from the kids into mailbags. We numbered the bags and the officers made Kaspar Snit and Slouch carry them outside and put them into the trunk of the squad car. The policeman told Slouch and Kaspar Snit to get into the backseat. Kaspar Snit ducked his head, saying, "You haven't seen the last of me, Eleanor Blande."

"Be quiet, you," said the policeman. "Or I'll tell you some knock-knock jokes."

We all waved as the police car drove away.

"Wait a minute," said the actor who played the dad on *The Zoomers*. "Does this mean our show is canceled?"

"Look on the bright side," Solly said. "Nobody will be bugging you for autographs anymore."

Mrs. Leer came home with us, as she was not going off until the next day. I was so grateful to fall into my own bed that I fell asleep in about half a second and didn't wake up until late in the morning. The rest of my family was already at the breakfast table, admiring a big photograph on the front page of the newspaper. A photograph of me flying. Because it was taken from the television, the picture was blurry and, with the goggles over my eyes, you couldn't tell it was me. Under it was a headline in giant type: MYSTERY FLYING GIRL CAPTURES KASPAR SNIT.

It told the story of how Kaspar Snit tried to steal the million dollars from well-meaning children, and how a girl with the power to fly defeated him. It quoted an expert in "preteen behavior," who called me a positive role model and said that "parents need to recognize their children's special gifts, whether it be creative writing, science, trick bike-riding, or flying."

Under the main story, there was another: WHO IS MYSTERY FLYING GIRL? *SENTINAL* OFFERS ONE THOUSAND DOLLAR REWARD.

"Uh-oh," said Mom. "I don't like the sound of this."

"I can't see, I can't see," Solly said. "Read it out loud." So my mother did.

JUST WHO IS THE MYSTERY GIRL IN OUR MIDST, THE EXTRAORDINARILY TALENTED YOUNGSTER WHO APPEARS TO BE ABLE TO LIFT INTO THE AIR, HOVER, SWOOP, AND EVEN DO SOMERSAULTS? UNLESS, OF COURSE, HER AMAZING TELEVISED FEATS WERE A CLEVER OPTICAL ILLUSION, PERFORMED WITH THE HELP OF A PROFESSIONAL MAGICIAN, OR PERHAPS ACHIEVED WITH DIGITAL COMPUTER EFFECTS.

ASKED ABOUT THE PHENOMENON, SCIENTISTS IN THE AEROSPACE DEPARTMENT OF NEARBY RUSTY COLLEGE COULD OFFER NO CONVINCING EXPLANATION AND EXPRESSED THEIR DOUBTS THAT A HUMAN BEING COULD ACTUALLY FLY. "PERSONALLY, I THINK SHE'S A FAKE," SAID PROFESSOR MORTIMER KEPP. "I THINK SHE'S DECEIVING THE PUBLIC, FEEDING

THEM FALSE INFORMATION. PRETTY SOON PEOPLE WILL BELIEVE IN GHOSTS AND BIGFOOT AND THAT THERE ARE ALIENS LIVING ON EARTH. PUBLIC MISCHIEF IS WHAT I CALL IT."

AND SO, ACTING IN THE PUBLIC INTEREST, THIS NEWSPAPER OFFERS A REWARD OF ONE THOUSAND DOLLARS TO WHOMEVER CAN REVEAL THE GIRL'S IDENTITY. THEN OUR REPORTERS CAN DETERMINE WHETHER SHE IS REAL OR NOT. IF YOU KNOW WHO THE MYSTERY FLYING GIRL IS, CONTACT THIS NEWSPAPER IMMEDIATELY.

"I can't believe it," I said, indignantly. "I'm not a fake."

"This is great," Solly said. "I can turn Eleanor in and get the thousand dollars."

"How could you even say that?" Mom asked. "You'll do no such thing. Eleanor is going to remain a mystery. She's going to stay a normal girl, right, Manfred?"

"Right, Daisy."

"But she isn't normal," Solly said. "She's the M.F.G."

"The what?" said Mom.

"The mysterious flying girl."

"Yes, she is normal," Dad insisted. "Having a . . . a special talent doesn't mean you're not normal. And besides, now that the amulet is gone, Eleanor won't be able to fly after the markings fade. So she really will be like everyone else."

I didn't say anything, but opened my hand to look at my palm. The outline markings were still there, thin but perfect.

It didn't look as if they were ever going to fade. Maybe they were going to stay forever. If that was true, then flying really had become part of who I was. I wanted to tell my parents – I knew that I should tell them – but somehow I couldn't get the words to come out of my mouth.

After breakfast, we all drove to the police station to arrange for the money to be sent to Verulia. But the police officer who liked to tell jokes had already taken care of everything. We rode to the airport in our car, along with a police escort flashing its lights and a police van holding the money. A special government plane was waiting to take the money to Verulia. Also waiting was His Excellency H. Waldorf Mansfeld, the ambassador from Verulia. He had come to escort the money to his country and to give us his official thanks. He stood in front of a giant glass window overlooking the runways and a plane marked AIR VERULIA. He had shiny hair, combed back, and a bristly little mustache. He wore a tuxedo with gray stripes down the trouser legs. His Excellency shook our hands and thanked us.

"This means a great deal to the Verulian people," he said, nodding. "We will send reports back of each new school and hospital and playground that we build. You and all the children have shown us that the rest of the world cares about Verulia."

"Can I make a suggestion?" Solly said.

"But, of course."

"You should use a little of that money to build a waterslide. Trust me, you'll be glad."

I said, "Excuse me, Excellency, but you look familiar."

"I do?" He looked at me and smiled. His smile grew bigger. And then I knew.

"You used to be the captain in Kaspar Snit's army! The one who wanted to be a ballet dancer. We met you at the fortress."

"I wondered if you would remember. Well, now I'm the ambassador. Pretty neat, huh? And once more you have helped us."

Over the loudspeaker came an announcement. *Last call for Air Verulia, flight 001.*

"I'd better go," said His Excellency.

"What happened to the ballet?" I asked.

"I dance in an amateur company. Let's just say, it is my version of flying."

He winked at me, turned around, ran, and did a beautiful *jeté* before going through the gate.

Mrs. Leer sent her letter of resignation by special delivery. She said that it would reach the Union of Extraordinary Caregivers by tomorrow. She spent the afternoon preparing to leave and Solly and I helped pack her trunk and heft it onto her little car. Mrs. Leer tried to cheer us up with stories from her travels, but Solly and I were feeling pretty glum at the thought of her resignation. We weren't even cheered up by the sight of Julia and Jeremy Worthington taking out the trash. On the very top of the trash can were all their Zoomer toys – the dolls, the clothes, and even the Zoomer house.

"Why are you throwing them out?" Solly asked.

"Haven't you heard?" said Julia. "The show's been canceled. Nobody wants Zoomer dolls anymore."

"Yeah," said Jeremy. "Plus they broke really fast. Instead of looking like they were flying, their heads started spinning around. And when you pressed the button on the mom, instead of saying, *I'm Zoomer-mom!* she said, *Ignatz your pundit!* Whatever that means."

We watched Julia and Jeremy go back in their house and then went to help Mrs. Leer tie the last rope around the trunk. "I still think it's rotten that you're resigning," Solly said. "Rotten, stinky, and putrid."

"Now, now, Solly," Mrs. Leer said gently. "Let's just say, I'm taking early retirement. Will the two of you write to me? None of that e-mail nonsense; I mean a real letter in an envelope, written in your own hand. And now, I really must be off. I need big hugs from the both of you. And, oh, what's in my eye? A little speck, that's all, getting me all watery."

Mom and Dad came out of the house to say good-bye too.

"It is an excellent fountain you have. I wish the dear, dreary Mr. Leer had seen it," Mrs. Leer said, standing by her car. "He had an eye for shapely marble. Well, I'm off. I wish you all the very, very best."

Slowly the little car drove away and we watched until it disappeared around a corner.

"Are we ever going to see her again?" I asked.

"I hope so," Mom said.

But I couldn't just forget about Mrs. Leer – or that she was resigning when Solly's capture and then ours wasn't her fault. So, on the next night, which was Sunday, I got out the map to see how far it was to Winnipeg, the North American office of the I.U.E.C. It was pretty far, but because of the time zones, Winnipeg was one hour earlier than we were. That meant that if I started out really early, I could, with luck, make the morning meeting and get back before my parents knew I was gone. So I set my alarm for 5:00 A.M., went to sleep, and found myself awake ten minutes before the alarm was supposed to ring. I dressed without making any noise, crept into the living room, opened the window, and took off into the early morning.

The flight was long and I passed over acres of wheat fields, but nothing eventful happened. At last I came to the outskirts of Winnipeg, half an hour behind schedule. I headed downtown and found the I.U.E.C. office, an old four-story corner building covered in ivy. I landed in the bushes of a park across the street, straightened my clothes, and hurried over.

The reception-room walls were decorated with bright paintings and collages by kids. I went right up to the secretary at the front desk. She told me the disciplinary committee was meeting in the boardroom on the fourth floor, but that it was a closed session and nobody could go in. I said thank you and, when she bent down to look for something, I raced up the stairs. I was so breathless that, when I reached the boardroom door, I had to stop for a moment. Through the door's oval window, I could see eight women and four men at a long table. At one end was a man with a very long beard, who was cleaning his spectacles and talking. I put my ear to the door.

"In light of this significant breach of regulation 143, subsection D, I propose that we accept the resignation of Lucretia Leer. Yes, I know her record until now has been impeccable, but the code is very clear. It is time to vote. All those in favor . . ."

I gritted my teeth, opened the door, and walked in.

"Wait," I said.

I was almost an hour late getting back, and it was already light by the time I was over our street. Fortunately, nobody seemed to be outside yet, except for a couple of sparrows drinking from the base of our fountain. They made me think of Kaspar Snit covered in feathers and I had to smile. I wondered how he was doing in jail. I sure wouldn't have wanted to be his cell mate. Well, he'd probably figured out a way to get the guards to do all his chores for him.

Now I began to make my descent, adjusting the angle to slide through the open window, and closing my eyes until my feet touched the carpet. It was a relief to be home again.

I heard a noise.

"Ahem."

Oh, no. I opened my eyes and saw Mom, Dad, and Solly, all with their arms crossed as they stared at me.

"Oh, hi," I said. "I went to get the newspaper and locked myself out of the house. Silly me. I had to climb in the window."

"I didn't see any climbing," Dad said. "I saw floating, or drifting, or landing – whatever you want to call it."

"Yeah, mystery girl," Solly said.

"Eleanor, what's going on?" Mom asked, taking a step towards me and looking into my eyes. "The amulet has been lost. Your markings should have faded by now. How is it you can fly?"

They were all looking at me with that same question in their eyes. It was as good a time as any to tell them. Or rather, show them. "Look," I said. "Look at my palm." I held it out for them to see.

"Hey, you've still got the markings," Solly said, jealously.

"But they're different," Mom said. "They're just the outline."

"Let me see," Dad said. "Eleanor, what does this mean?"

"I don't exactly know. A little bit of outline stayed each time until it was all there. I can fly with it."

"And when is it going to fade?" Dad asked.

"It isn't fading. Not at all."

Mom gasped. "You mean, it's *permanent*?"

"Looks like it." I gave an embarrassed smile.

"What do you mean, permanent?" Solly said. "Like a permanent marker that never comes off? You mean, Eleanor can fly whenever she wants, forever? And we can't fly at all? It's not fair!"

"I didn't do it on purpose."

"We wanted you to be normal," Dad said.

"She still is normal," Mom said, although she sighed. "I guess she's just a normal flying girl."

"Well, there are still going to be rules about flying in this house," Dad said. "Just because you have a bike doesn't mean you can ride wherever you want, whenever you want. Right, Daisy? There have to be rules."

"Of course, there have to be rules," Mom said. And then under her breath, she whispered, "You're so lucky."

"I know," I whispered back and giggled.

16

UNDERWATER UNDERWEAR

After dinner one Saturday night, my father read to us an article in the back pages of the newspaper.

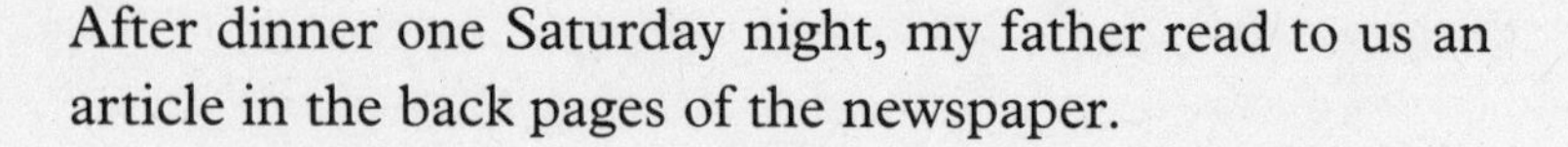

REWARD FOR FLYING GIRL STILL UNCLAIMED

IT HAS BEEN A MONTH SINCE THE *SENTINAL* OFFERED A REWARD OF ONE THOUSAND DOLLARS TO ANYONE WHO COULD REVEAL THE TRUE IDENTITY OF THE MYSTERIOUS FLYING GIRL WHO HELPED TO DEFEAT KASPAR SNIT AND SEND ONE MILLION DOLLARS TO THE PEOPLE OF VERULIA. PERHAPS HER IDENTITY WILL NEVER BE DISCOVERED. HOWEVER, OUR OFFER STILL STANDS.

MEANWHILE, A REPORT FROM THE WARDEN OF THE PRISON HOLDING KASPAR SNIT STATES THAT THE MAN WHO ONCE DECLARED HIMSELF AN "EVIL GENIUS" IS PROVING TO BE A WELL-BEHAVED INMATE. "KASPAR SNIT," WRITES THE WARDEN, "IS CONSIDERATE, POLITE, AND HELPFUL TO OTHER INMATES. HE PERFORMS HIS DUTIES AS ASSISTANT LIBRARIAN WITH GENUINE ZEAL. HE HAS EXPRESSED SINCERE REGRET AT HIS FORMER BEHAVIOR. IF HE CONTINUES TO BEHAVE HIMSELF, I WILL RECOMMEND TO THE PAROLE BOARD THAT KASPAR SNIT BE GIVEN AN EARLY RELEASE."

"I don't know," Mom said. "He fooled us before. He might be trying to fool everyone again. What do you think, Eleanor? You seem to know him best."

Did I know him best? I thought that maybe he was sincere and maybe he was also faking it. He might be a bit sorry, but he might also be hoping to get out. I didn't get a chance to answer because Solly scooted into the room on his skate shoes, his PROPERTY OF HOTEL SCHMUTZ cape waving behind him.

"Hurry up, *The Swoomers* is almost on!" He zipped back around and went out again.

We followed him into the living room. *The Swoomers* was a new television show. Even before we had left Misery Mountain, the actors got a call on the Zoomer dad's cell phone. The executives of the studio wanted to replace the old show with a new one. The actors would play a family of superheroes with the ability to breathe underwater like fish. It didn't sound nearly as good an idea as a flying family, at least to me, but they were happy to get the new jobs.

The television network had rushed the show into production to take advantage of all the publicity surrounding the actors and their release from the clutches of Kaspar Snit. We all sat around the living room, Solly with G.W. on his shoulder, like always. Mom turned on the television.

THE SWOOMERS
STARRING

On a beach a man jogged onto the screen in a tight-fitting superhero outfit, but this time it was blue. He looked out at the ocean and smiled.

Rupert Musk as GEORGE SWOOMER

A woman in a matching superhero outfit jogged up beside him, her cape waving behind her. She, too, scanned the ocean.

Elizabeth Jenkens as LILY SWOOMER

Then the camera pulled back a little and two kids in superhero outfits ran up to their parents, who hugged them. They all toppled into the sand.

Featuring Stevie Levine as GEORGE, JR.
and Amanda Devine as FRANCINE

Solly said, "How come they couldn't even think of new names?"

"Shh," the rest of us said. Just then the picture cut to the bottom of the ocean. A black submarine rocked gently in the water. Then we were inside the sub, in a laboratory of smoking and bubbling vials. There was Slouch in a black cape. He'd been arrested too, but the judge had agreed to let him go to the studio, accompanied by a guard. On the screen, he looked up and straight into the camera with a playful glint in his eye, as if to say, *See? Slouch always lands on his feet.*

And Marvin Slouch as THE EVIL KARY SNEAK

At least they changed *his* name. The image of the evil Kary Sneak faded to neon-colored fish swimming past a coral reef. Onto the screen swam Lily Swoomer and the kids, George, Jr. and Francine. It didn't look like they were really underwater; it looked like there was a piece of blue plastic over the camera lens.

Solly said, "Do you think they're wearing special underwater underwear?" The camera went up to the surface and there was the dad, George Swoomer, struggling along in a rowboat.

"Hey!" George shouted, "Wait for me!"

Dad groaned. "Is he going to say that every week?"

★

At bedtime, Mom and Dad called me into Solly's room. I sat in my pajamas on the edge of his bed while my parents looked at us both.

"Whatever we did," Solly said, "it was all Eleanor's fault."

"You didn't do anything wrong," said Dad. "On the contrary. Read it to them, Daisy."

Mom pulled a letter from her pocket. "It's from Mrs. Leer," she said. "It came this morning."

My dearest Eleanor, Solly, Mr. Blande, and Ms. Galinski,

Well, I do not know what you did, but the disciplinary committee of the I.U.E.C. refused to accept my resignation. At first, I was going to insist, but then the committee told me of a position in which my services were badly wanted. A family of seven children, very wild, needing to be attended for a month. And so I am off to Lima, Peru, in an hour's time.

As the dear, dreary Mr. Leer used to say, it is good to feel that one is needed. My deepest thanks. Love to you all until we meet again.

Your devoted nanny,
Lucretia Leer

"Well done, Eleanor," Dad said. I smiled and thought how lucky those seven kids in Peru were.

*

The moon woke me up. It was full and round and a silvery light streamed in through my window. I couldn't help but get up and look outside.

I could see a cat walking across the top of a roof and the shape of a kite caught in a tree. It was such a beautiful night, I just couldn't resist going for a little flight. I listened for a minute, but didn't hear anything. Carefully I got out of bed, went out my door, shutting it behind me, and tiptoed to the living room. And there I saw Solly and Mom. They were standing in their pajamas, gazing out the open window.

"What are you doing up?" I asked.

"The moon," Solly said. "It's so big."

"Yes," said Mom, wistfully. "Solly and I were just talking about what a lovely night it is for flying. I guess that's why you're here, Eleanor."

I nodded. "I'm sorry that we lost the amulet; that I'm the only one who can fly. I wish you could fly too."

"It's not your fault," Solly admitted.

I came up beside them and we all looked out the window. "I guess you're the last of the flying Galinskis. First my grandmother, then my mother, and then me. And you're the end of the line."

For a while, nobody said anything. Then I started thinking. I opened my palm and looked at it in the moonlight. You had to look closely to see the outline, but there it was – the faintest pale violet.

"Solly," I said. "Give me your hand."

"I don't feel like holding hands."

"I want to try an experiment. Press your palm onto mine."

"I don't see what that will do," he said, but he held out his hand and I put mine on top of his.

"Yuck, your hand is sticky," I said. "Push harder."

Mom looked at us. "Eleanor?"

Slowly I let go of Solly's hand. "Let's see," I said.

"I don't want to look," Solly said. "It would be too disappointing."

"Come on." I took his hand and Mom and I both peered at it closely. We could see a faint outline.

"It's there!" I said. "See it, Mom?"

"I do. Here, Eleanor, press my hand."

I did and then we checked Mom's hand too. The outline of the moon and three stars was on her palm.

"I'm going to try," Solly said. "Give me some room."

Mom and I took a step away. Solly closed his eyes, put his hands at his sides, tilted up his chin, and breathed in deeply. He opened one eye and looked at me. "Here goes nothing," he said, and closed his eye again.

He rose onto his toes, stayed there a moment, and then his toes lifted ever so slowly off the carpet. He rose smoothly out the window.

"It works!" I cried. "It works!"

"*Shh,*" Mom said. "You'll wake your father. He can find out in the morning. Let's all go for a little trip, shall we?" Then she closed her eyes and, a moment later, she, too, was hovering in the night sky.

I was so glad not to be the only one of us who could fly again. I was about to join them when I heard a noise and turned around.

My dad was standing in the doorway.

"Oh, Dad."

He came over and put his hand on my shoulder. "You sure made them happy."

"I wish you could come, too."

"Maybe you were right, Eleanor. Maybe I couldn't fly because I didn't really want to. But I guess I feel differently now. I wish I could fly. But go on, you don't want to be left behind."

"Dad?"

"Yes, sweetie?"

"Give me your hand."

"Well, I don't know. . . ."

"Do you really want to fly?"

Dad looked into my eyes. "Yes, I believe I do."

"Then what have we got to lose?"

Dad held out his hand. I pressed my palm into his, squeezing as hard as I could. I held his hand longer than Mom's and Solly's.

Dad took a deep breath. "Should we look?"

"Here goes nothing," I answered, my heart beating fast.

We let go. Dad turned his hand over. We both looked. Then we looked at each other, smiled, and turned to the open window.

CARY FAGAN is an award-winning children's author and writer of adult novels whose work has won the Mr. Christie Silver Medal, the City of Toronto Book Award, and the Jewish Book Committee Prize for Fiction. He is a contributor to a number of magazines and newspapers, including *The Globe and Mail, The Montreal Gazette,* and *Books in Canada.* In addition to several picture books, he wrote *Beyond the Dance*, a biography of the National Ballet of Canada's prima ballerina Chan Hon Goh, shortlisted for the Norma Fleck Award for children's non-fiction. His first children's novel, *The Fortress of Kaspar Snit*, was named a Silver Birch Award Honor Book. Cary Fagan lives in Toronto.